P9-CRK-102

JIMMY SNIFFLES THE SUPER-POWERED SNEEZE

Librarian Reviewer
Allyson A. W. Lyga, MS
Library Media/Graphic Novel Consultant
Fulbright Memorial Fund Scholar, author

Reading Consultant
Elizabeth Stedem
Educator/Consultant, Colorado Springs, CO
MA in Elementary Education, University of Denver, CO

STONE ARCH BOOKS
MINNEAPOLIS   SAN DIEGO

GN
F
NIC

Graphic Sparks are published by Stone Arch Books,
151 Good Counsel Drive, P.O. Box 669,
Mankato, Minnesota 56002.
www.stonearchbooks.com

Library of Congress Cataloging-in-Publication Data
Nickel, Scott.
The Super-Powered Sneeze / by Scott Nickel; illustrated by Steve Harpster.
p. cm. — (Graphic Sparks. Jimmy Sniffles)
ISBN-13: 978-1-59889-316-8 (library binding)
ISBN-10: 1-59889-316-5 (library binding)
ISBN-13: 978-1-59889-411-0 (paperback)
ISBN-10: 1-59889-411-0 (paperback)
1. Graphic novels. I. Harpster, Steve. II. Title.
PN6727.N544S86 2007
741.5'973—dc22 2006028026

Summary: Jimmy Sniffles' super powers lie in his nose. So what happens when his spectacular sniffs are wiped out by cold medicine? Nothing, and that's the problem. It sure would be disastrous if a super villain – say, Dr. Von Snotenstein – took advantage of Jimmy's weakness and escaped from the dream dimension. It would be even worse if the doctor had powerful Snot-Bot machine-terrors to help him conquer the world. Now that's nothing to sneeze at!

Art Director: Heather Kindseth
Graphic Designer: Brann Garvey

1 2 3 4 5 6 11 10 09 08 07 06

Printed in the United States of America

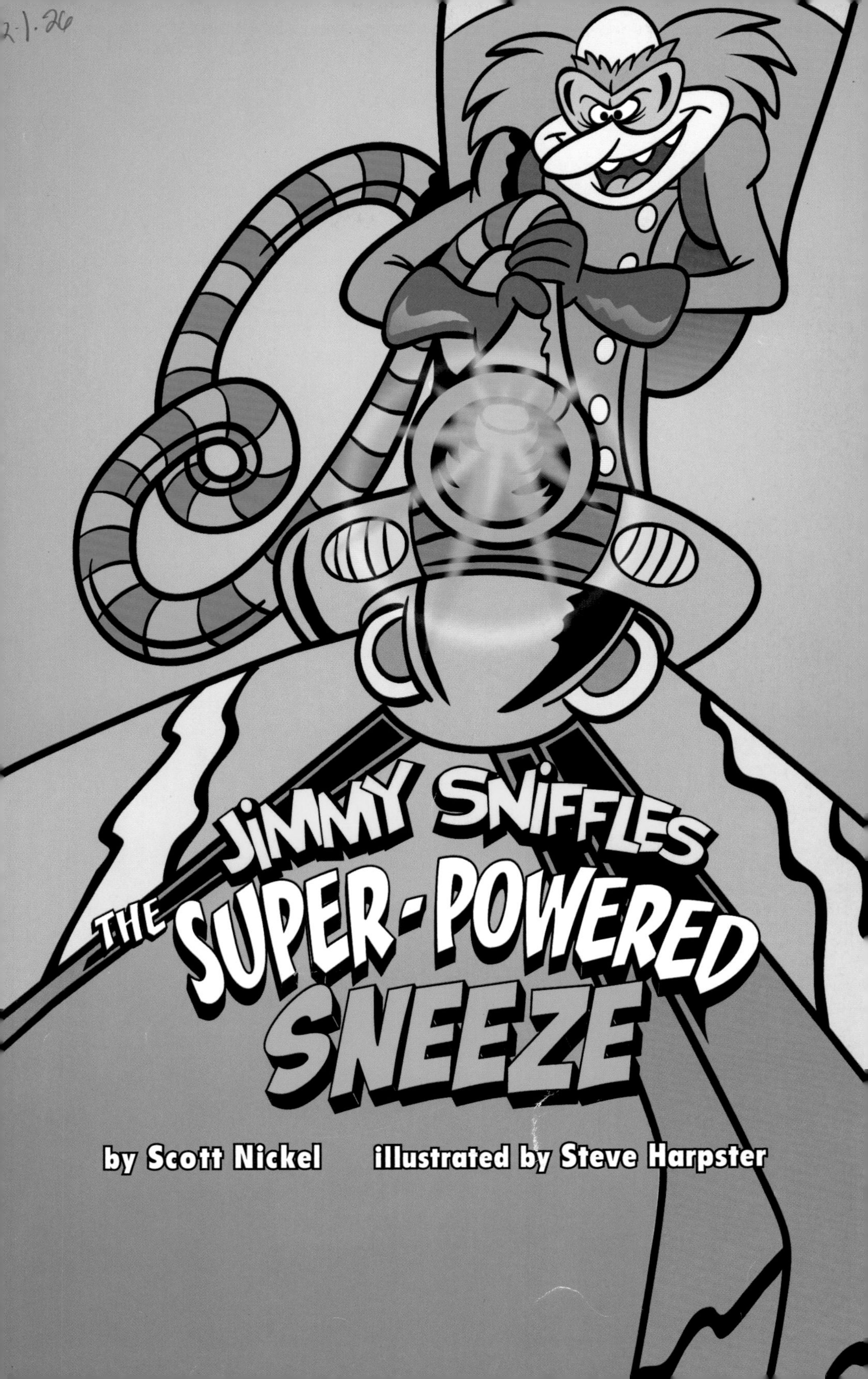

Jimmy Sniffles: The Super-Powered Sneeze

by Scott Nickel   illustrated by Steve Harpster

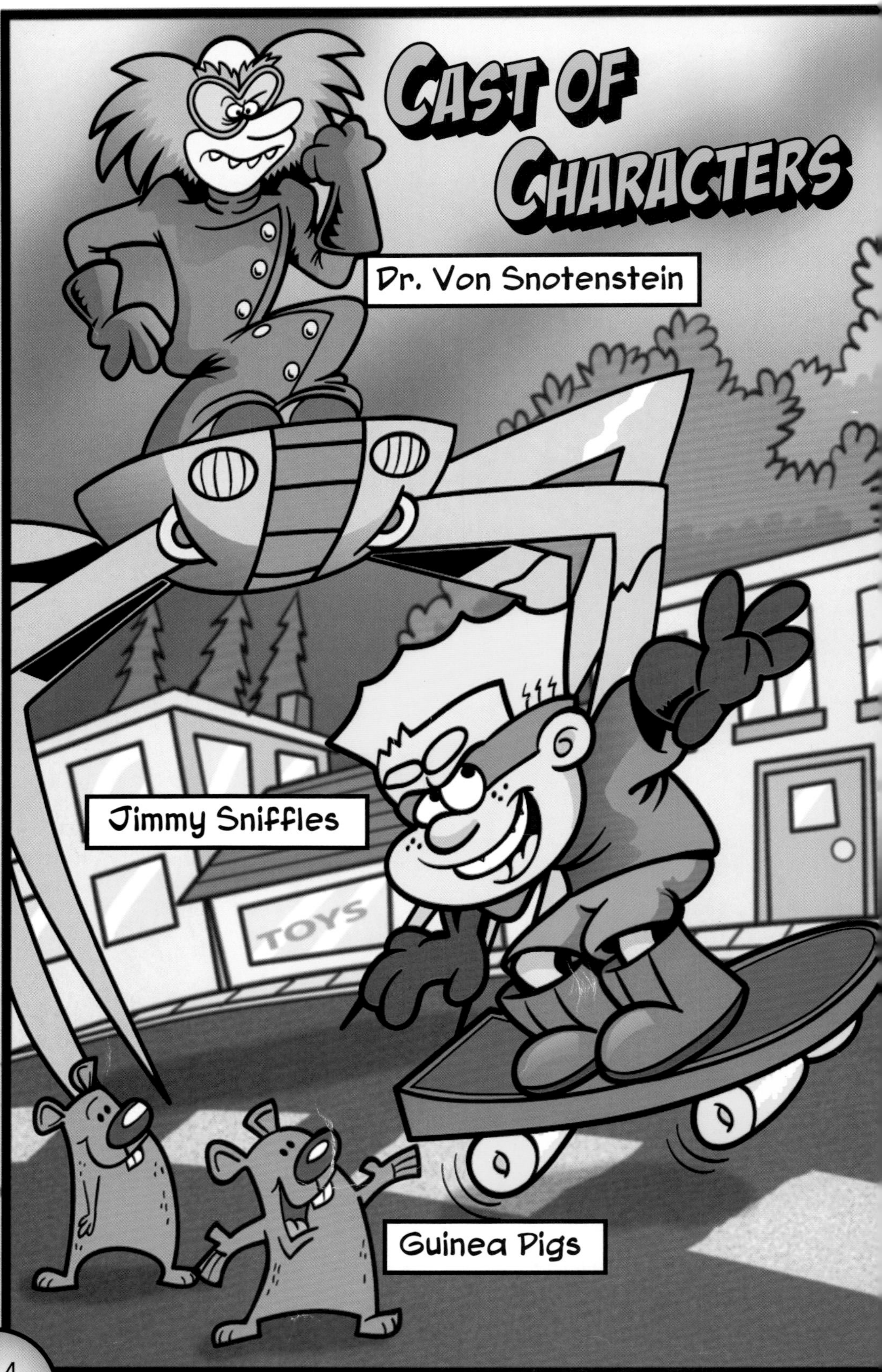
CAST OF CHARACTERS
Dr. Von Snotenstein
Jimmy Sniffles
TOYS
Guinea Pigs

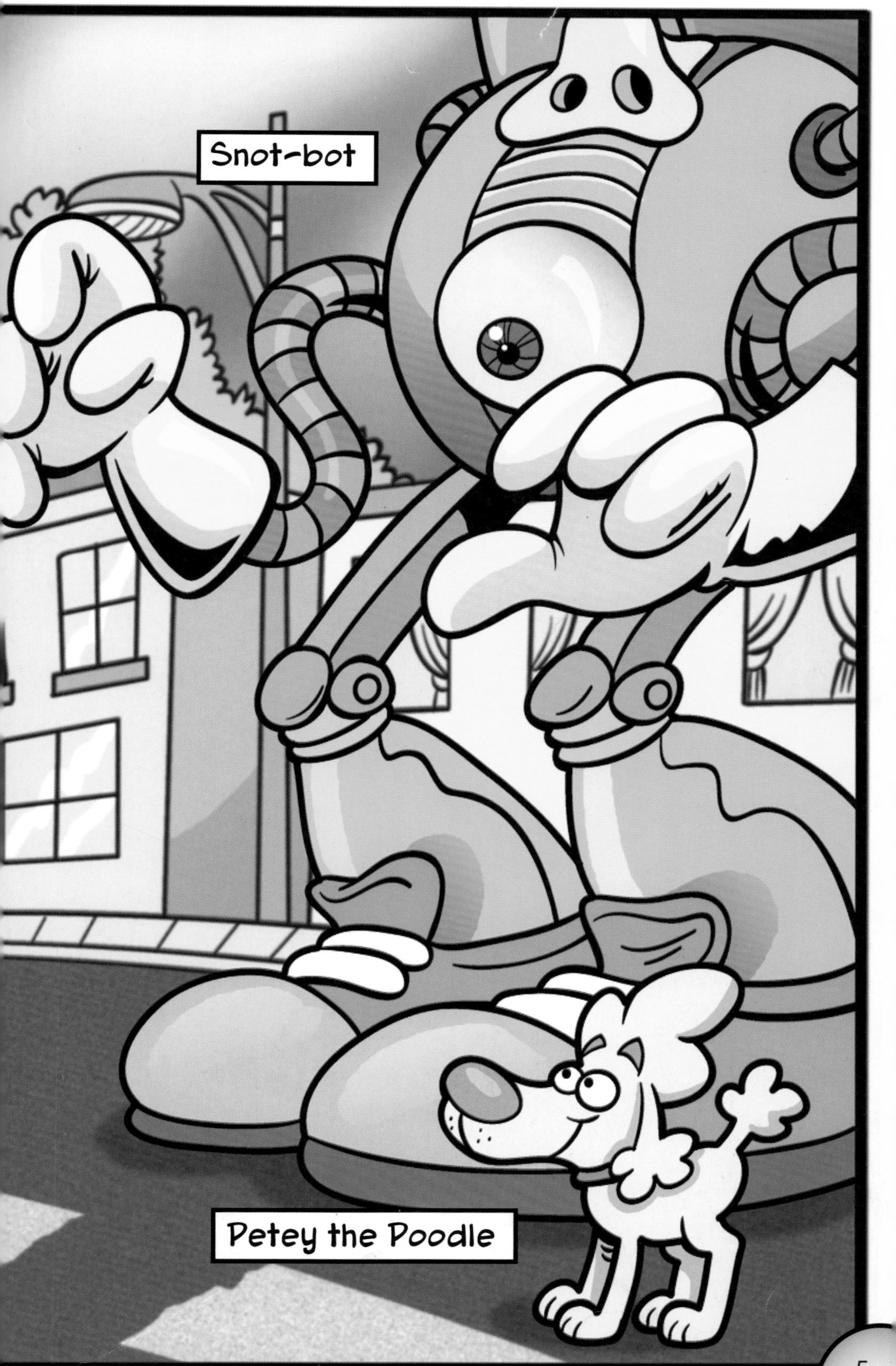
Snot-bot
Petey the Poodle

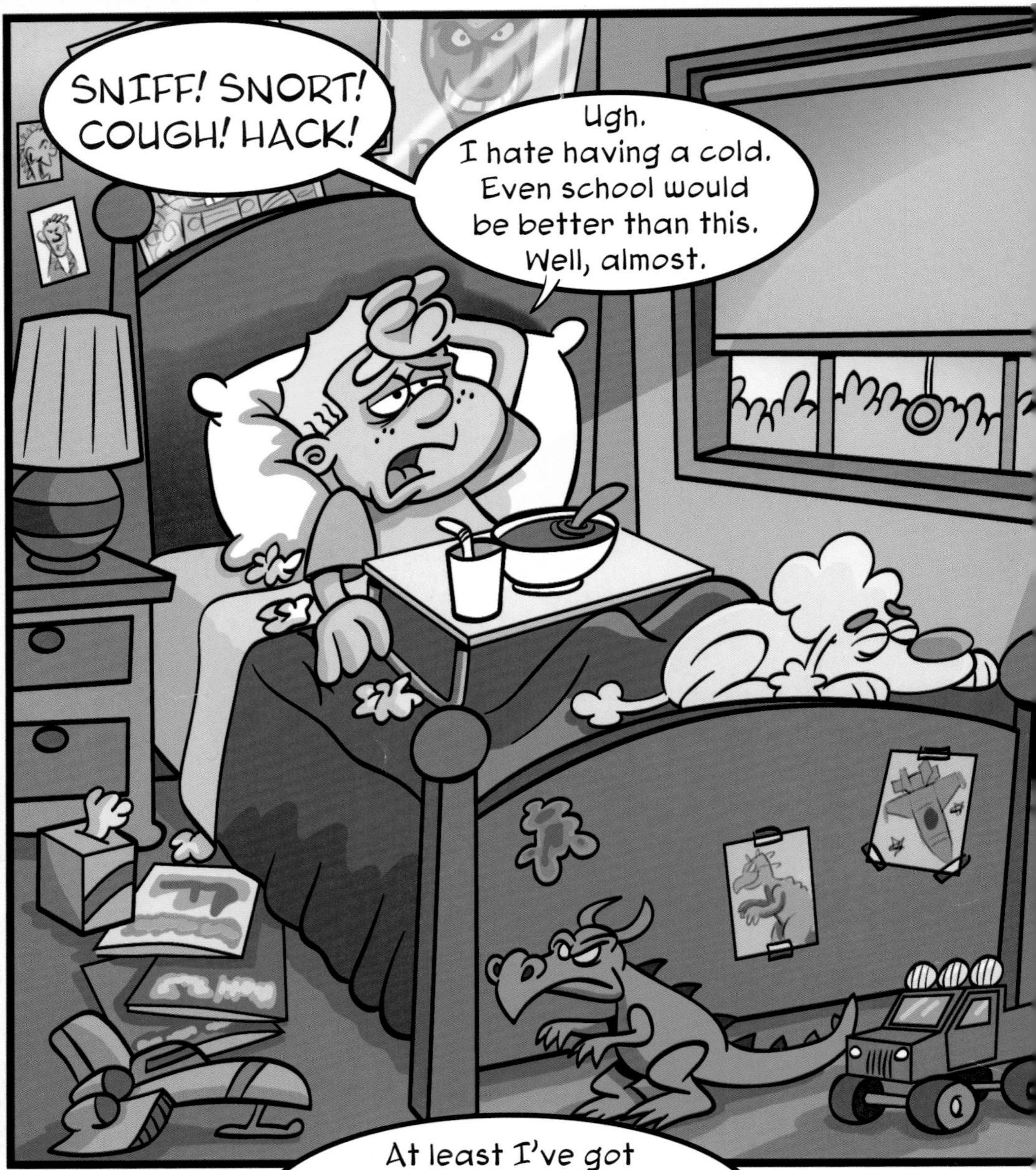
SNIFF! SNORT! COUGH! HACK!
Ugh. I hate having a cold. Even school would be better than this. Well, almost.

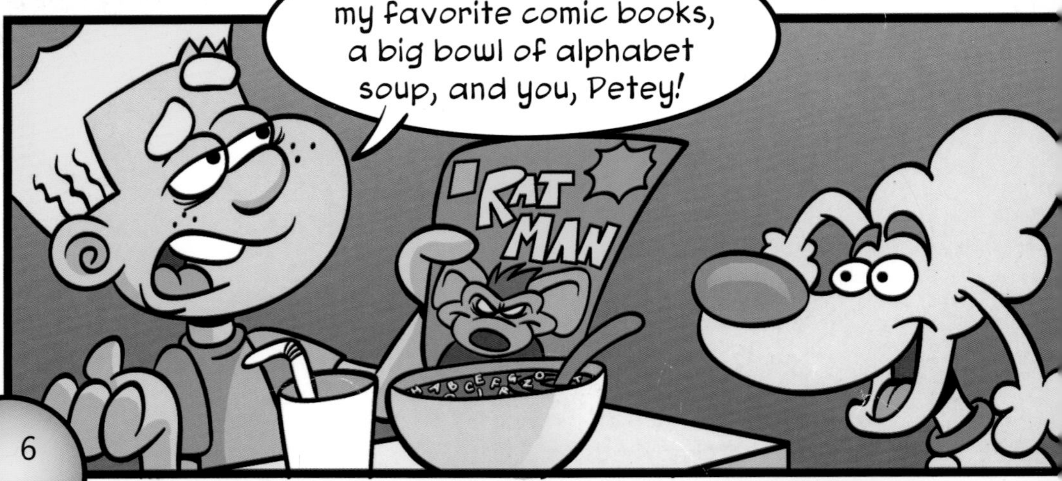
At least I've got my favorite comic books, a big bowl of alphabet soup, and you, Petey!
RAT MAN

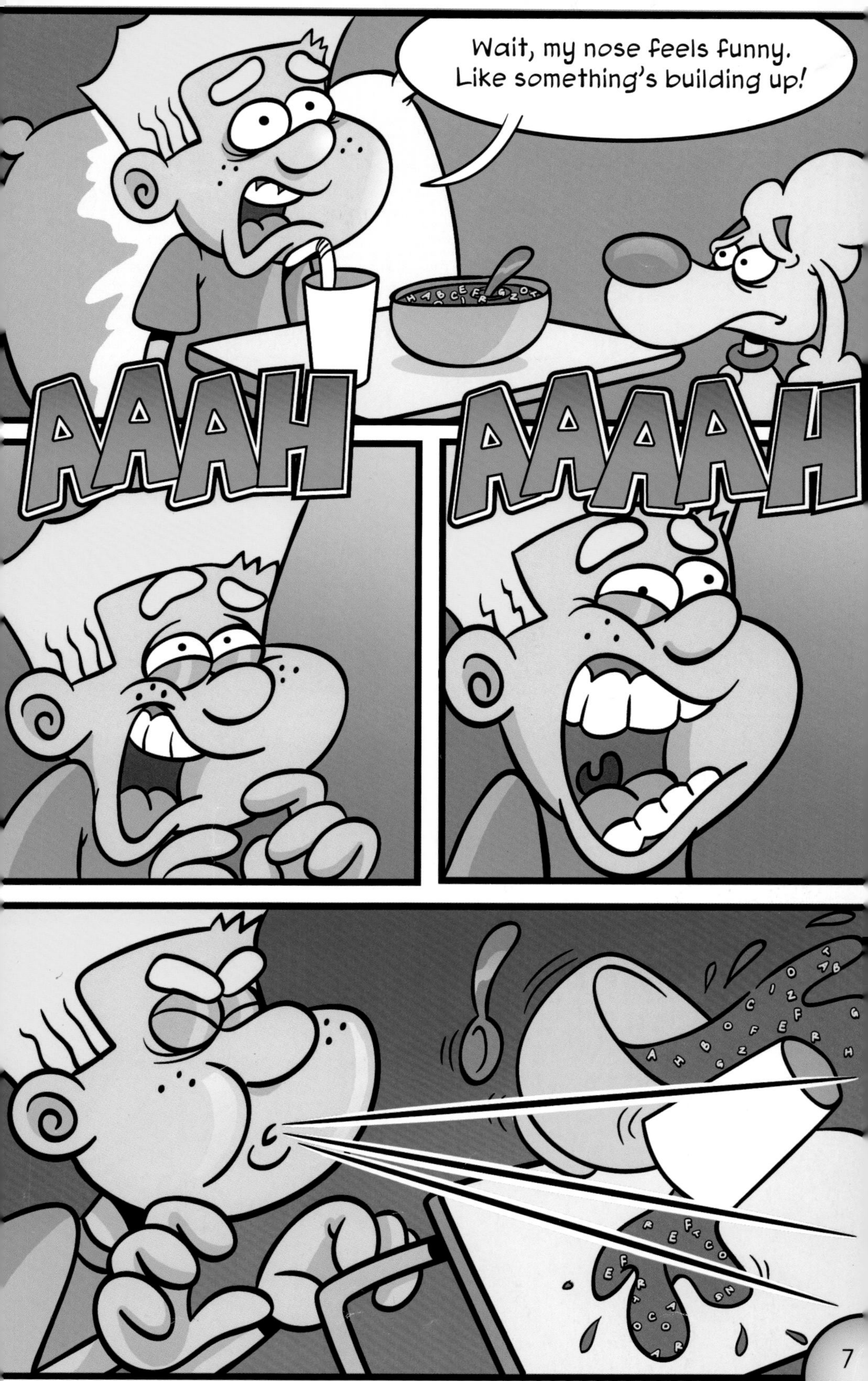
Wait, my nose feels funny. Like something's building up!
AAAH
AAAAH

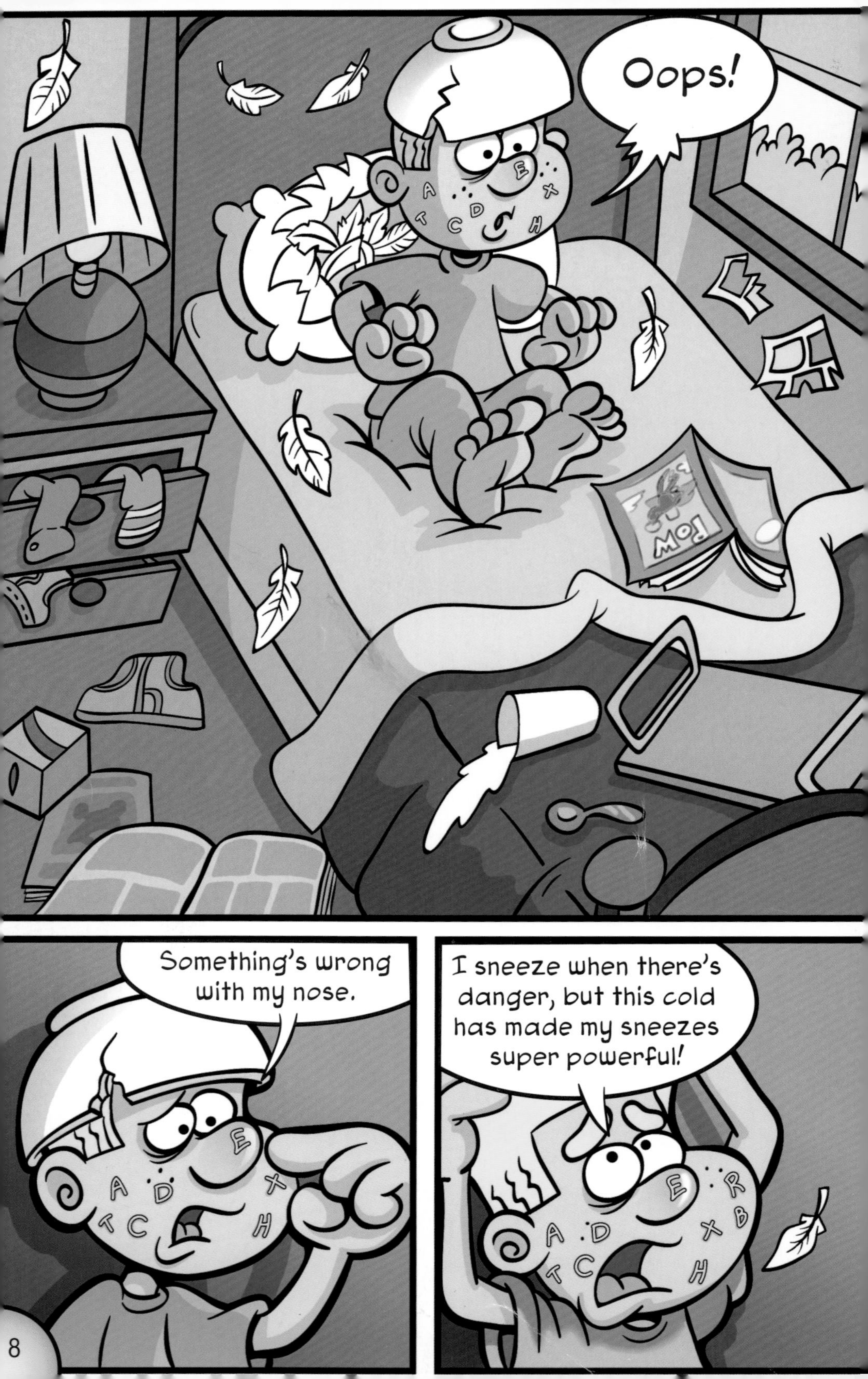
Oops!
Something's wrong with my nose.
I sneeze when there's danger, but this cold has made my sneezes super powerful!

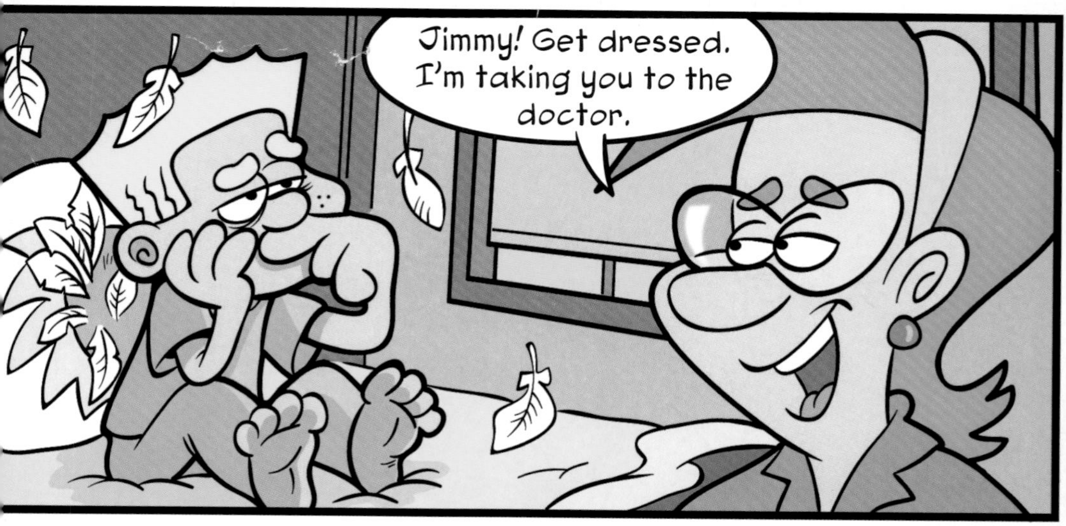
Jimmy! Get dressed. I'm taking you to the doctor.

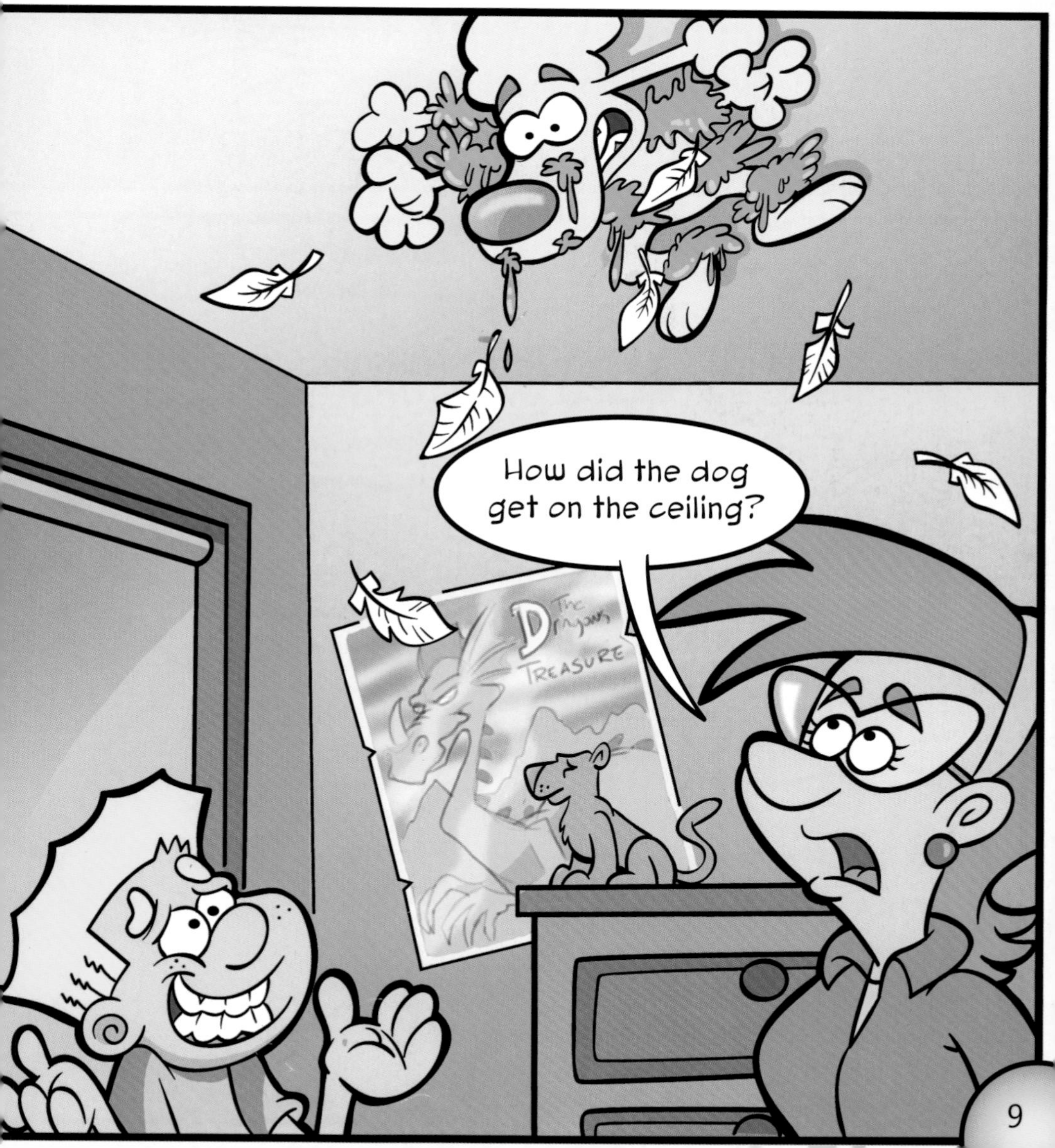
How did the dog get on the ceiling?
TREASURE

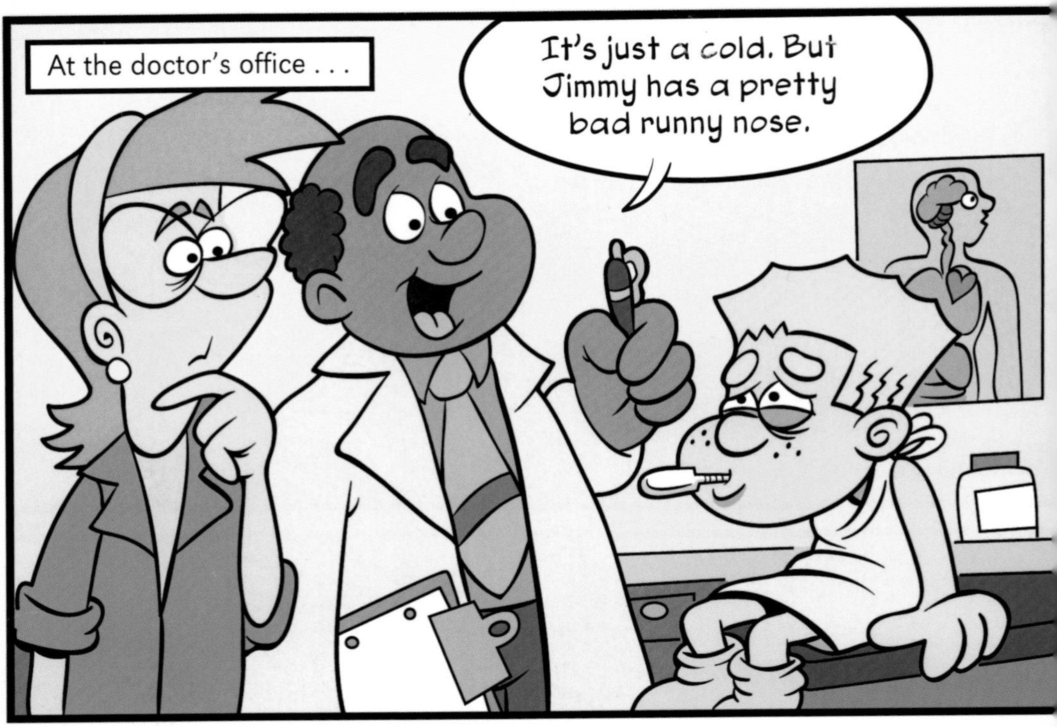
At the doctor's office . . .
It's just a cold. But Jimmy has a pretty bad runny nose.

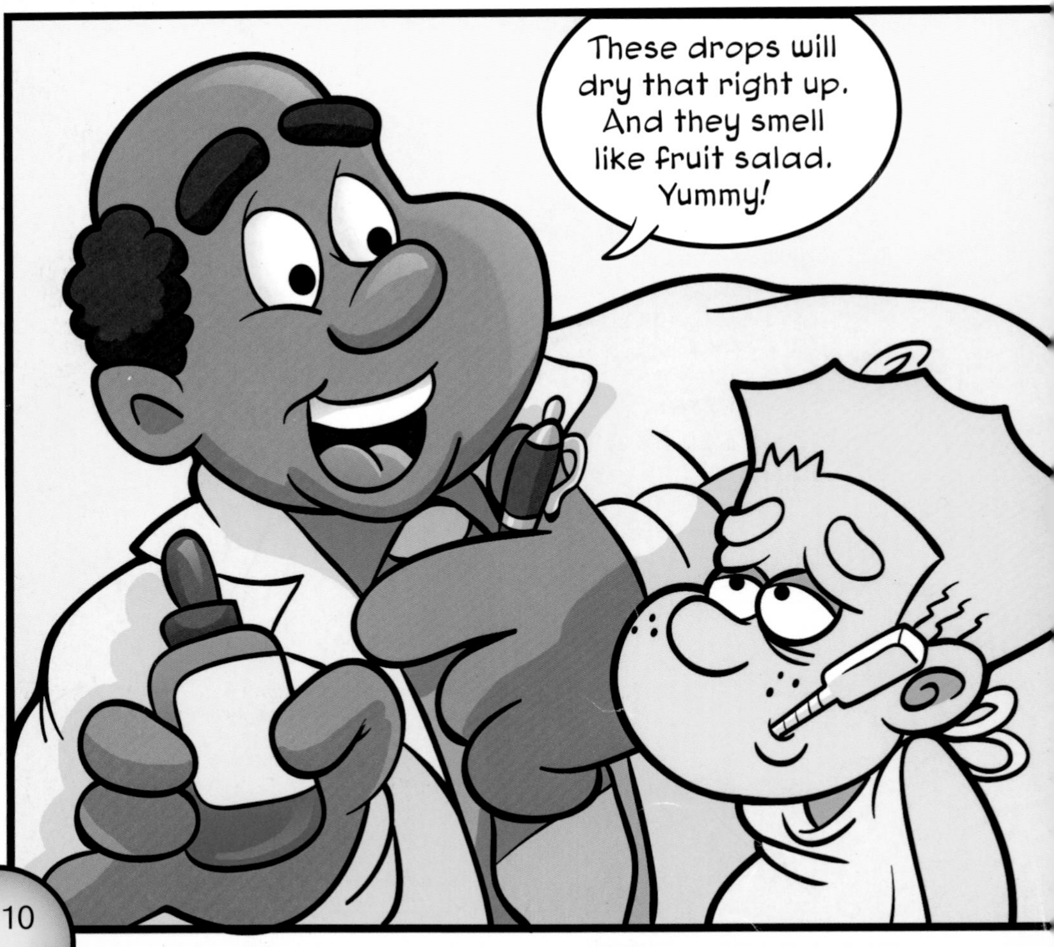
These drops will dry that right up. And they smell like fruit salad. Yummy!

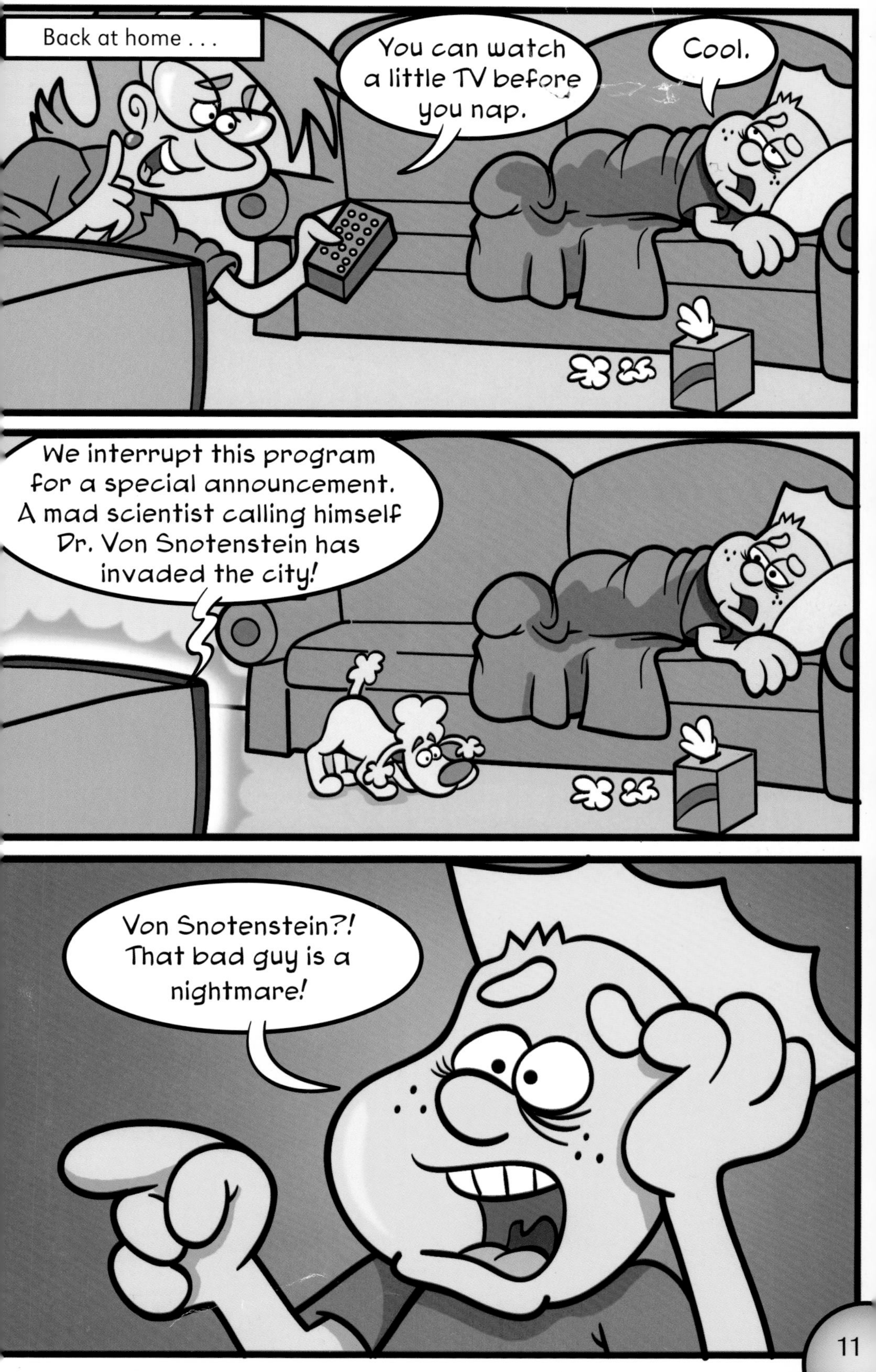
Back at home . . .
You can watch a little TV before you nap.
Cool.
We interrupt this program for a special announcement. A mad scientist calling himself Dr. Von Snotenstein has invaded the city!
Von Snotenstein?! That bad guy is a nightmare!

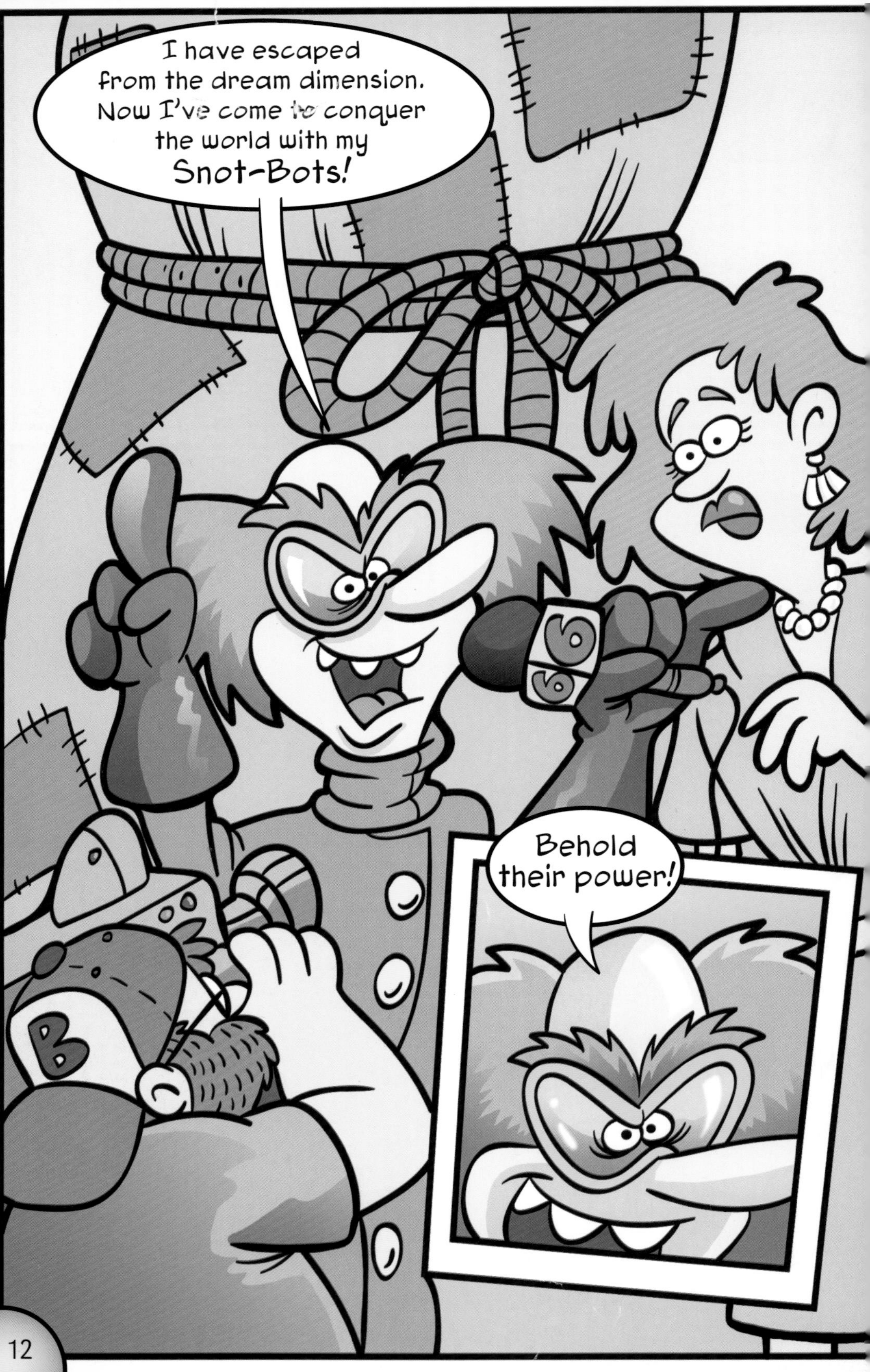
I have escaped from the dream dimension. Now I've come to conquer the world with my Snot-Bots!
Behold their power!

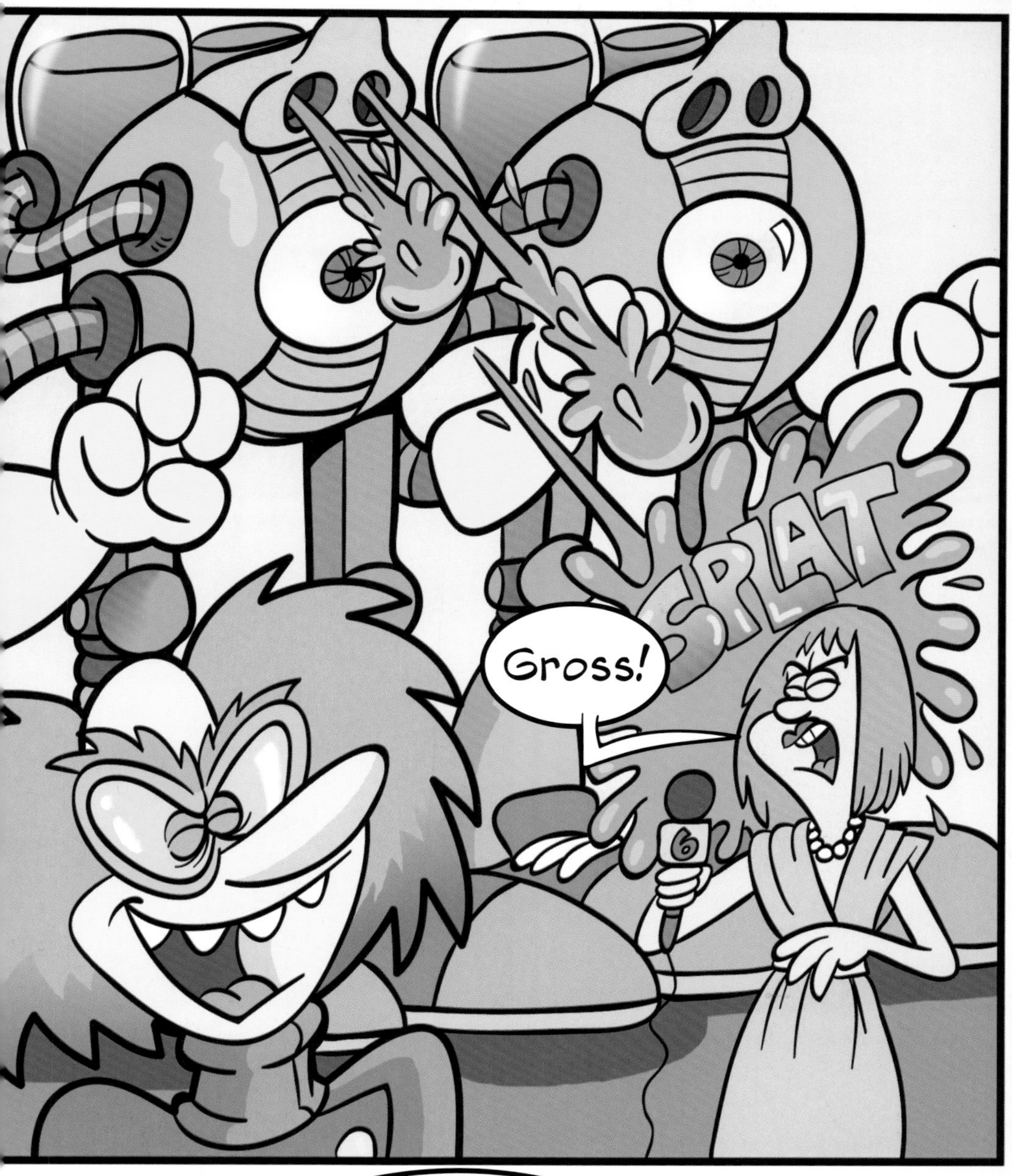
SPLAT
Gross!

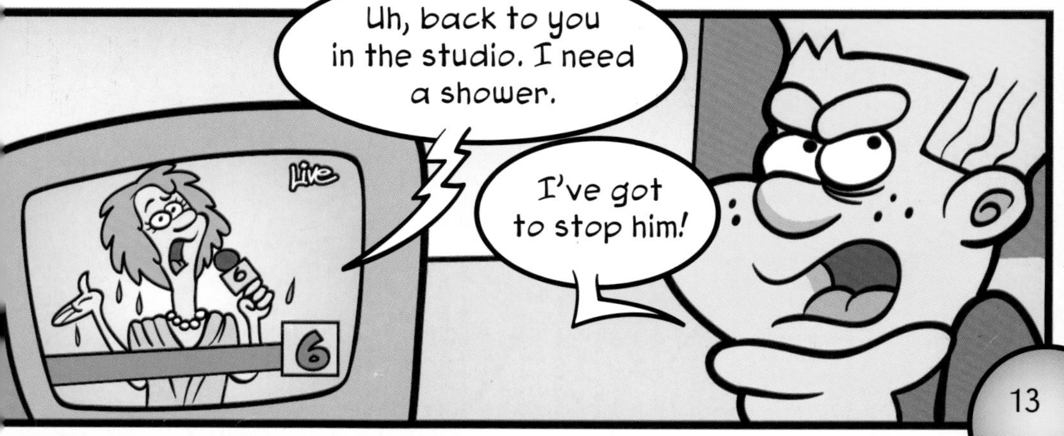
Uh, back to you in the studio. I need a shower.
I've got to stop him!
Live
6

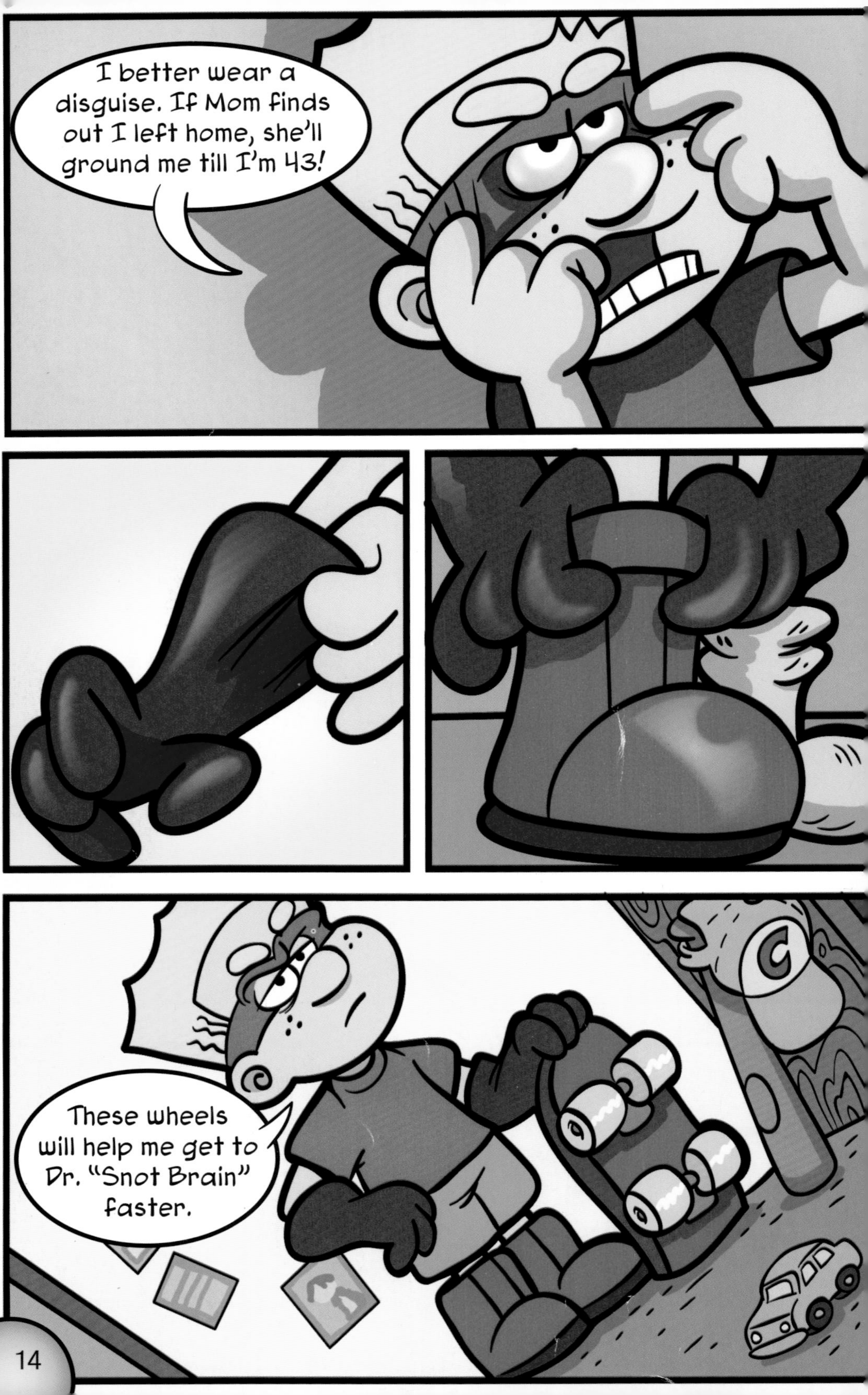
I better wear a disguise. If Mom finds out I left home, she'll ground me till I'm 43!
These wheels will help me get to Dr. "Snot Brain" faster.

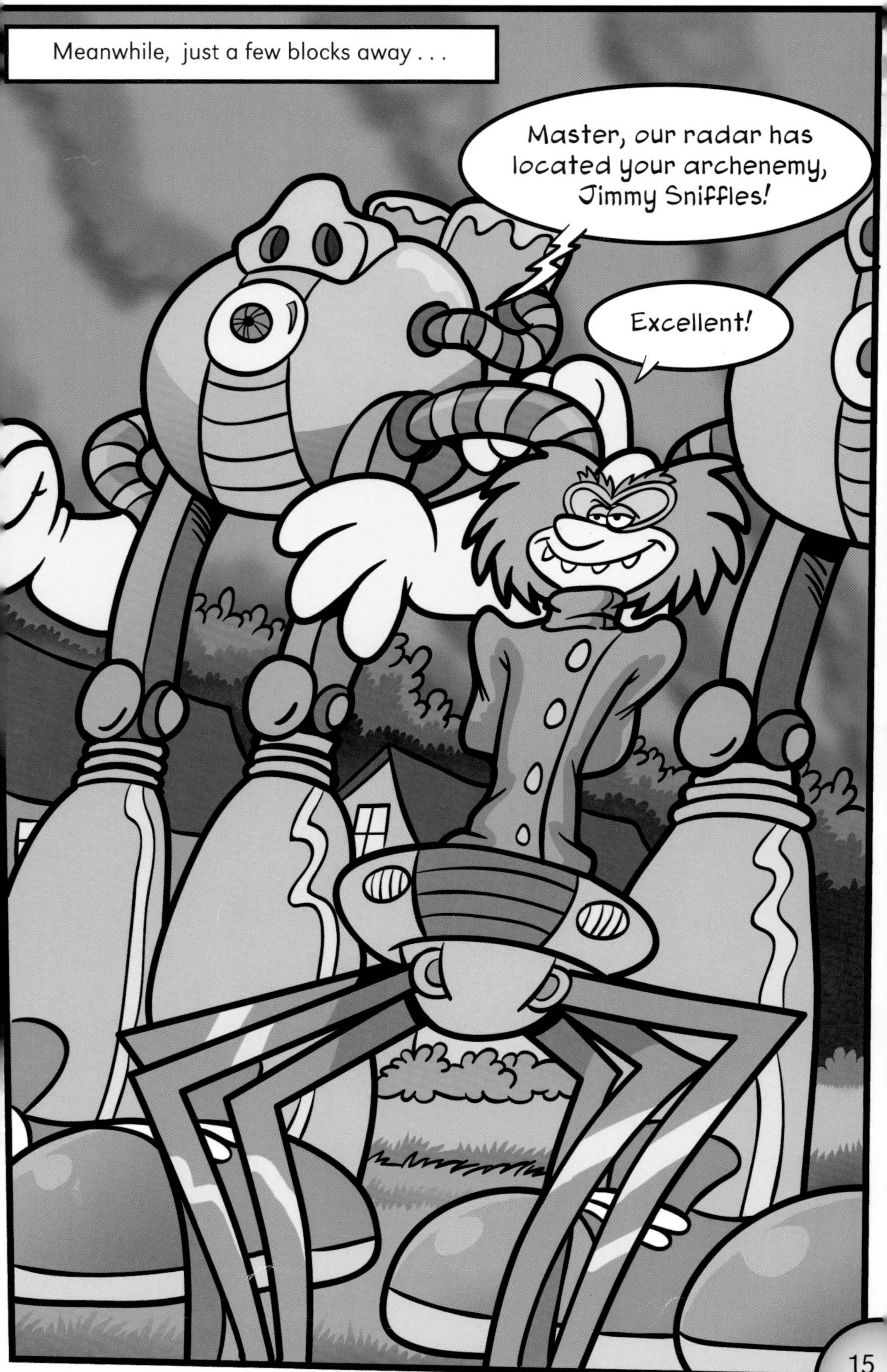
Meanwhile, just a few blocks away . . .
Master, our radar has located your archenemy, Jimmy Sniffles!
Excellent!

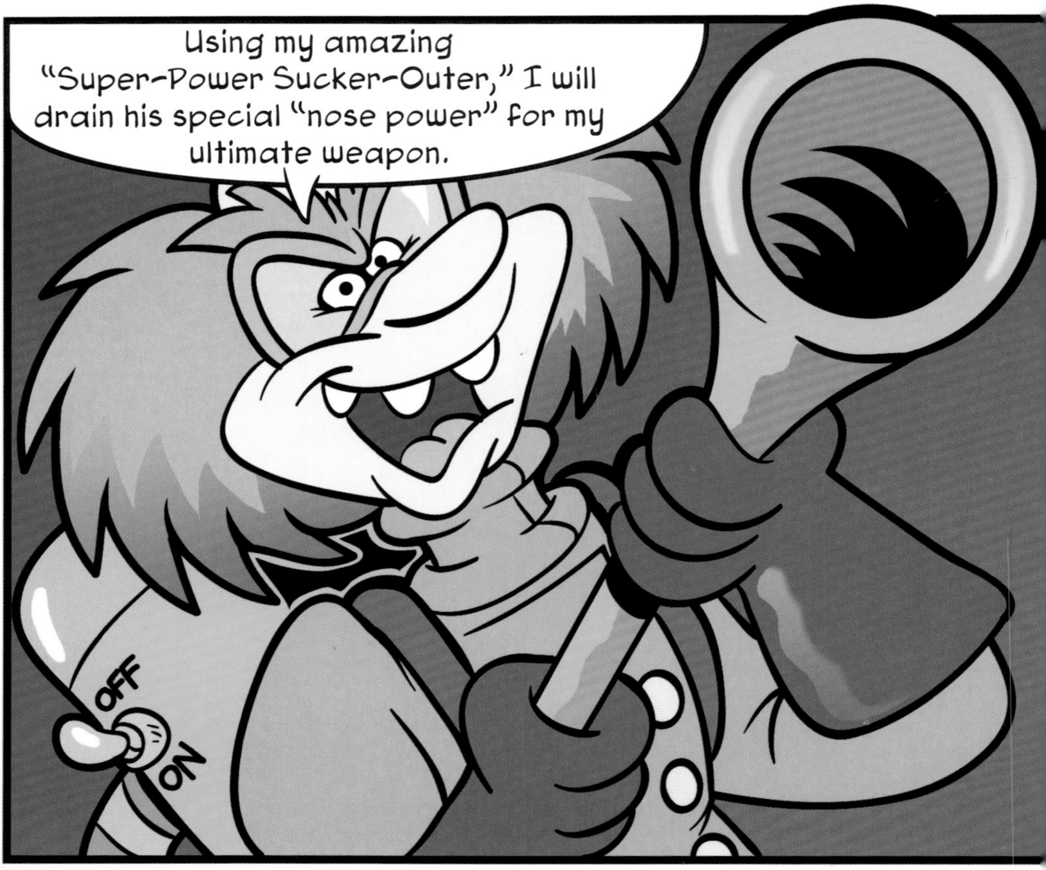
Using my amazing "Super-Power Sucker-Outer," I will drain his special "nose power" for my ultimate weapon.
OFF
ON

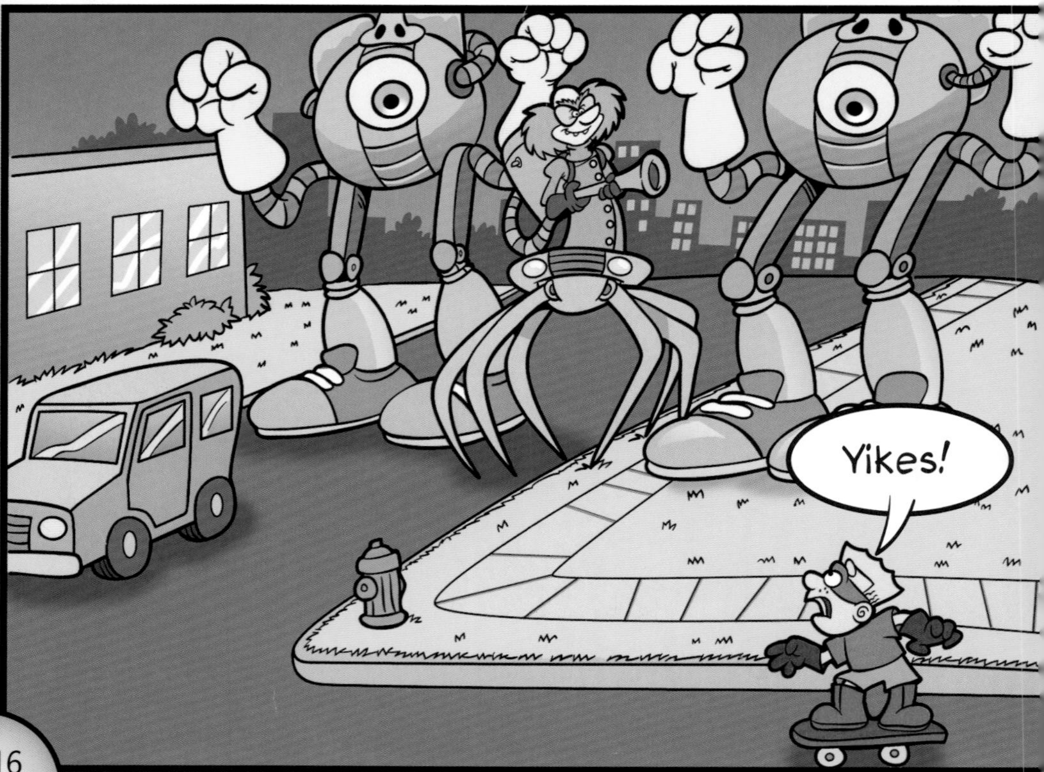
Yikes!

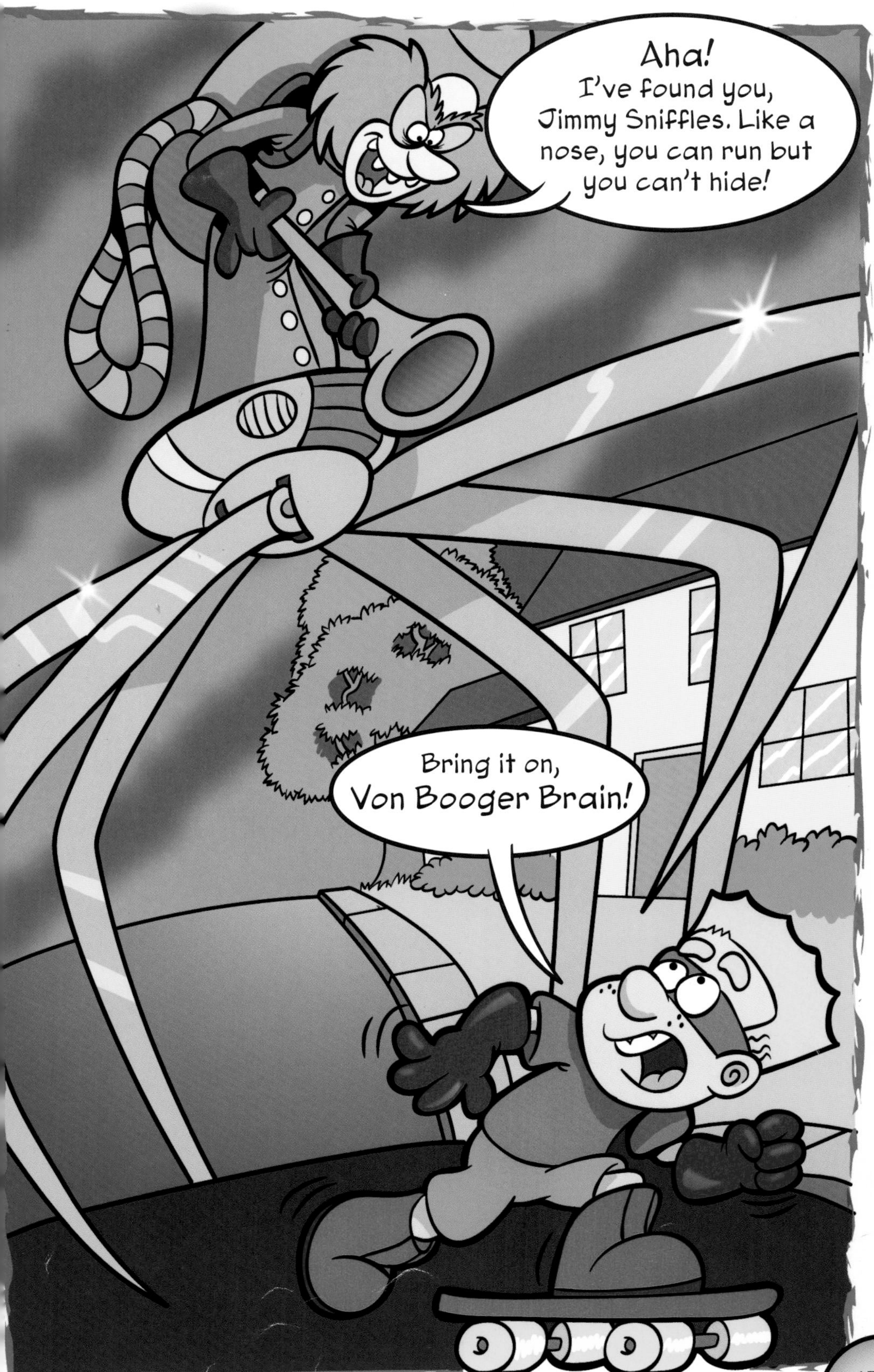
Aha! I've found you, Jimmy Sniffles. Like a nose, you can run but you can't hide!
Bring it on, Von Booger Brain!

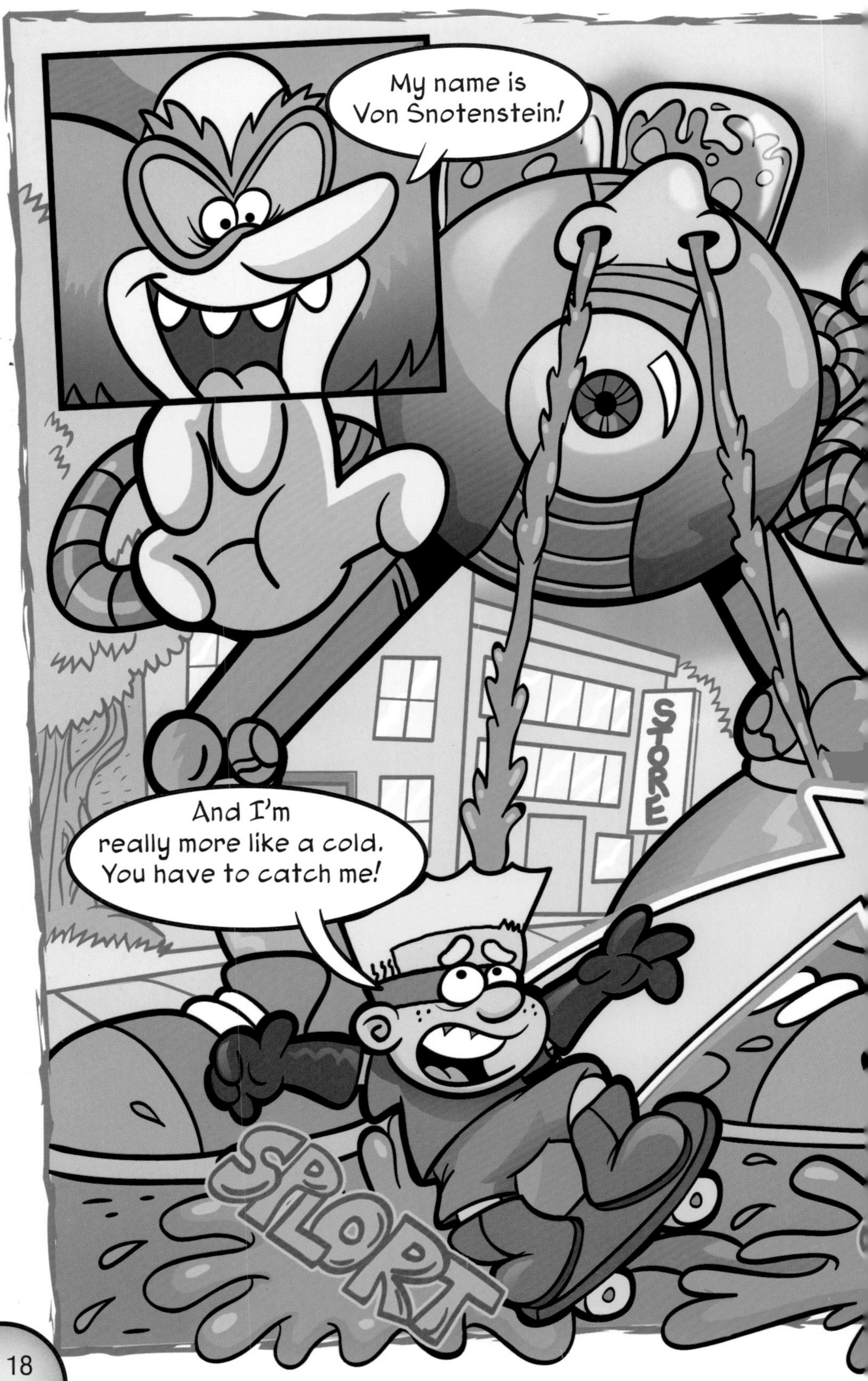
My name is Von Snotenstein!
STORE
And I'm really more like a cold. You have to catch me!
SPLORT

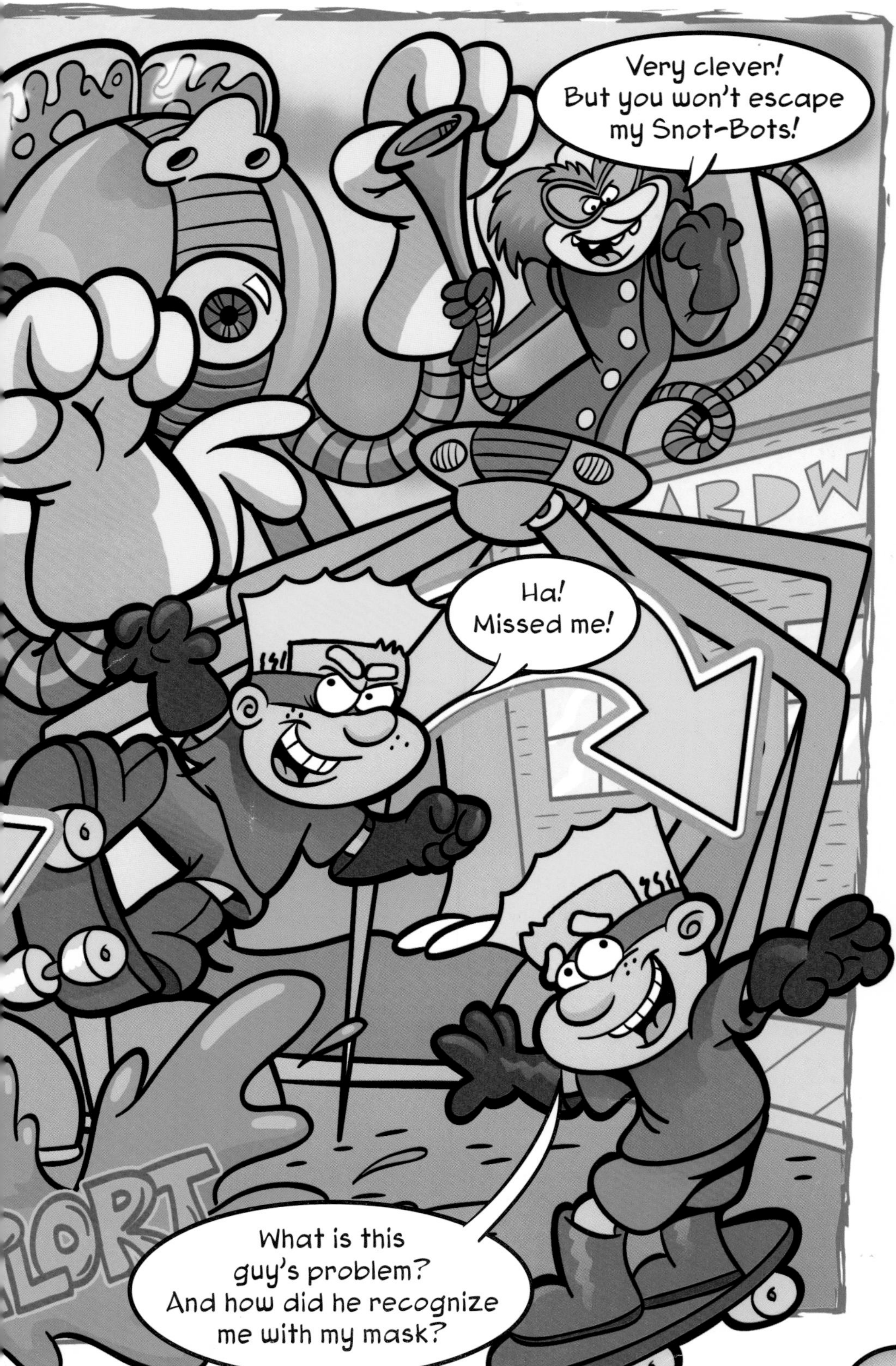

Very clever! But you won't escape my Snot-Bots!
Ha! Missed me!
What is this guy's problem? And how did he recognize me with my mask?

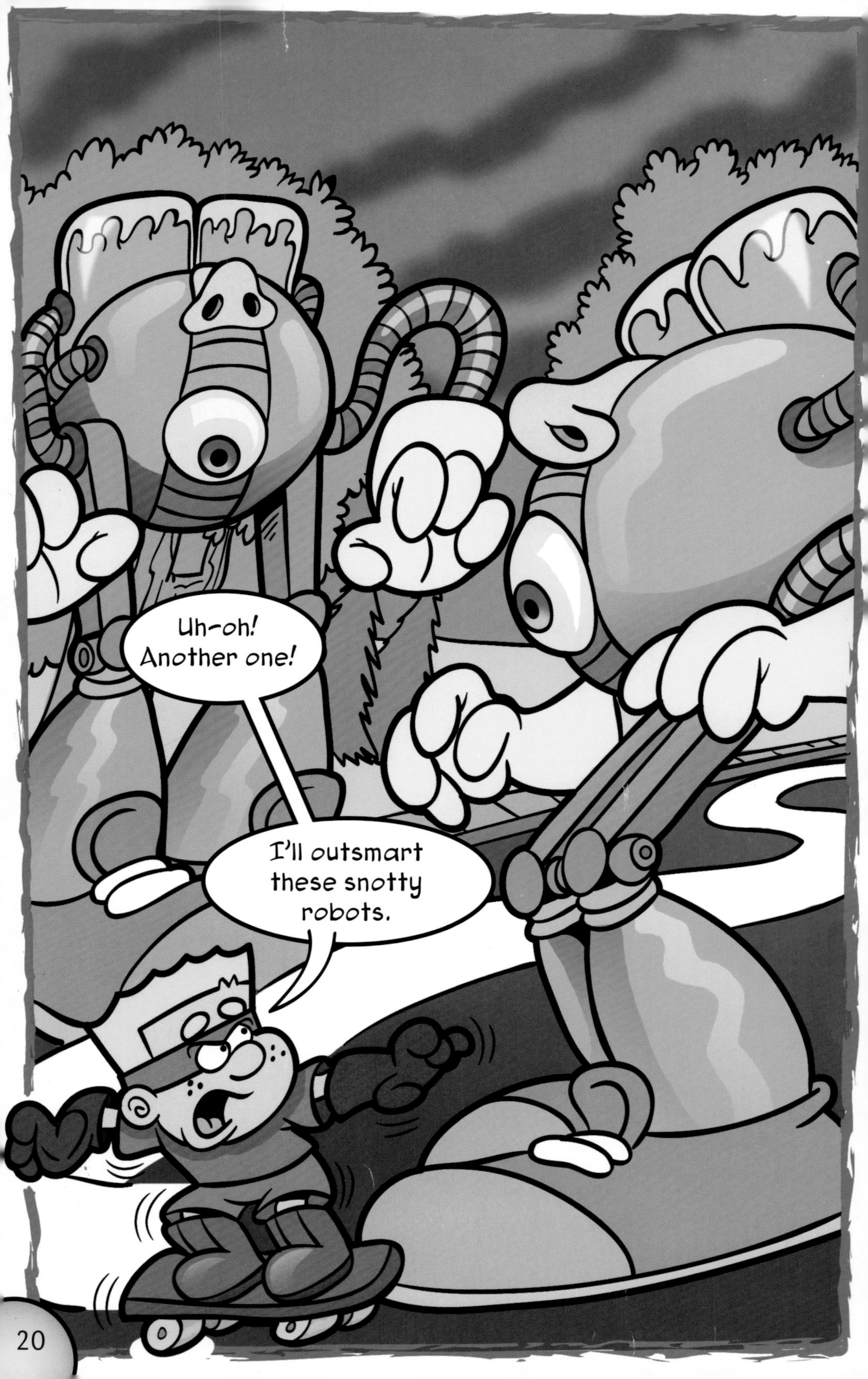
Uh-oh!
Another one!
I'll outsmart these snotty robots.

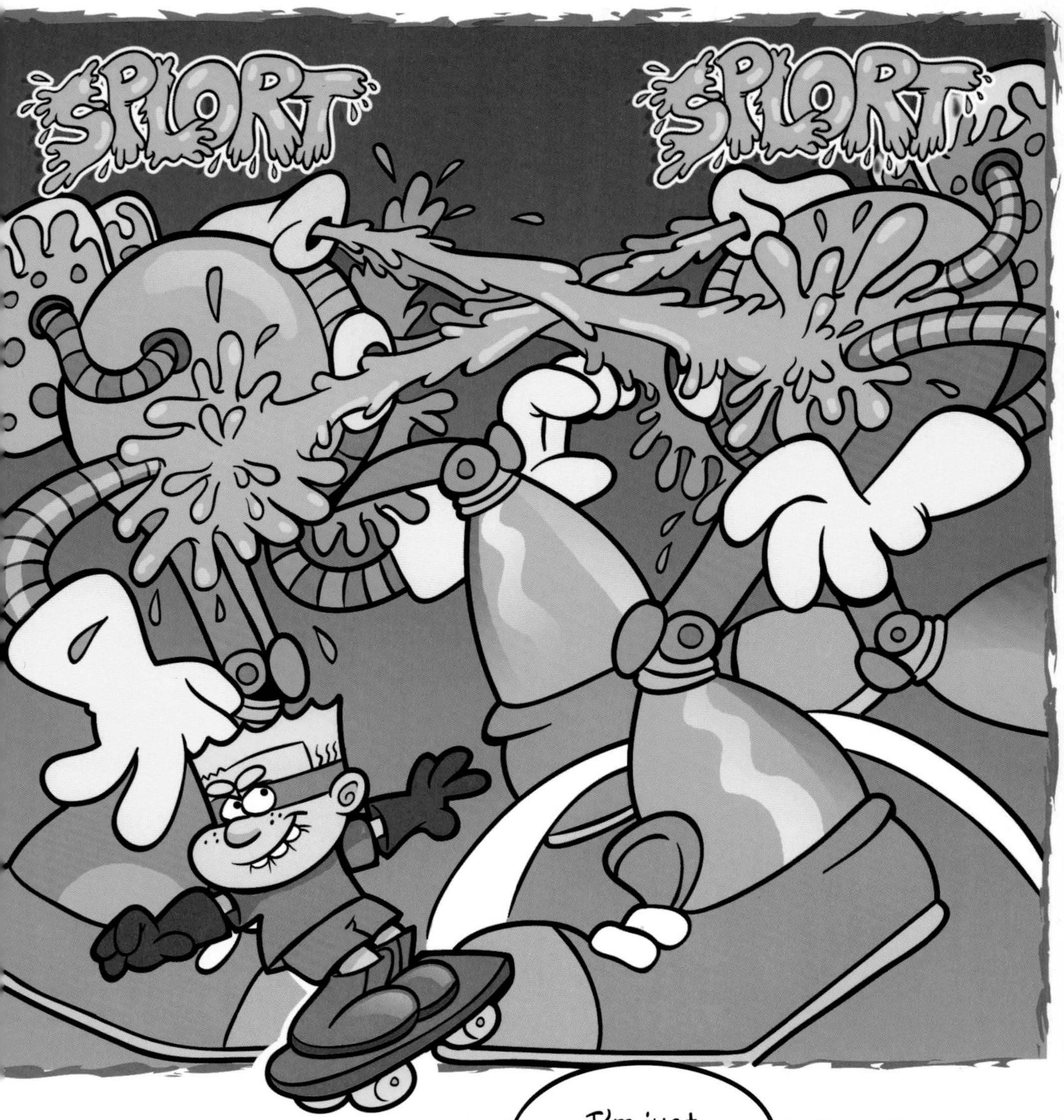
SPLORT
SPLORT

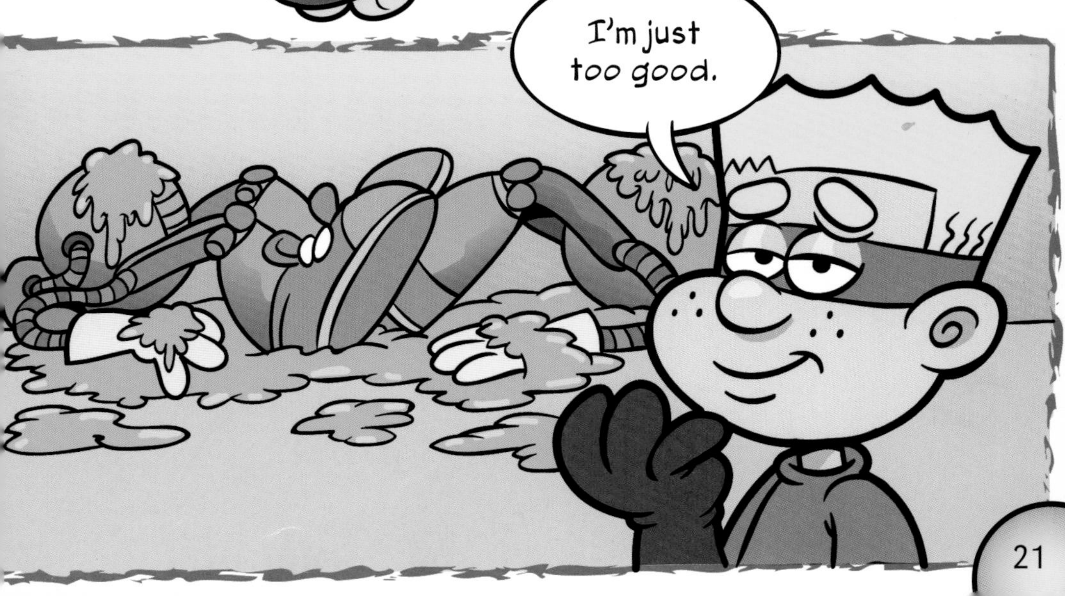
I'm just too good.

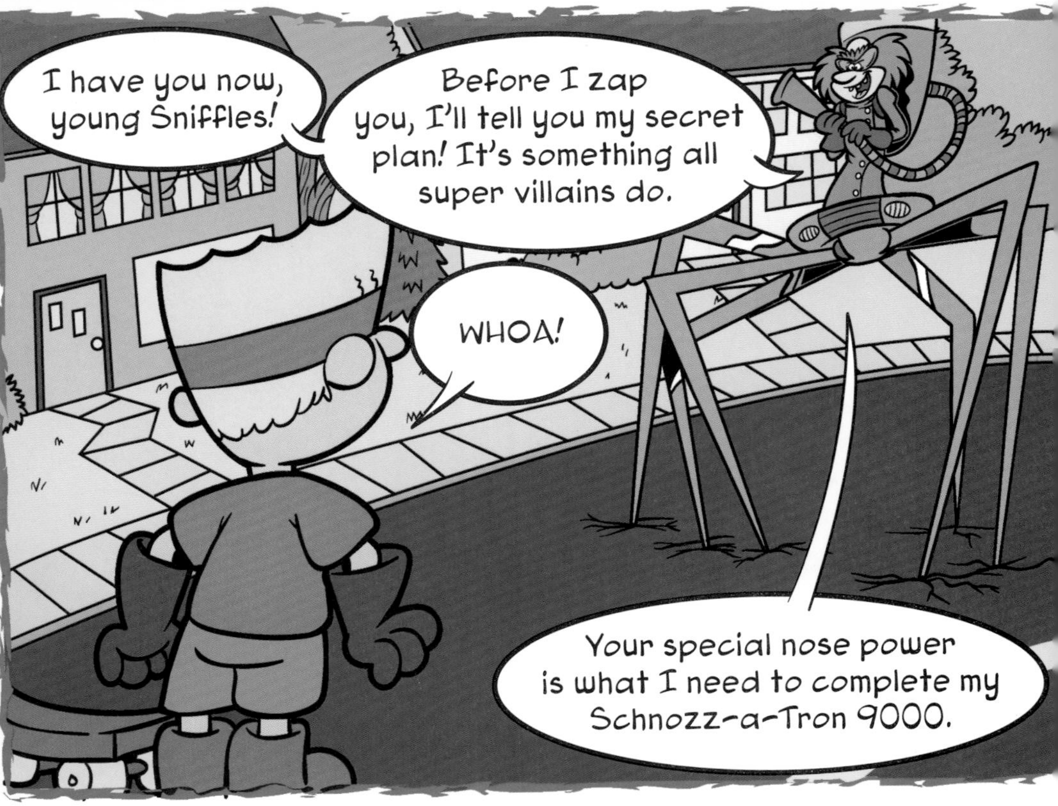
I have you now, young Sniffles!
Before I zap you, I'll tell you my secret plan! It's something all super villains do.
WHOA!
Your special nose power is what I need to complete my Schnozz-a-Tron 9000.

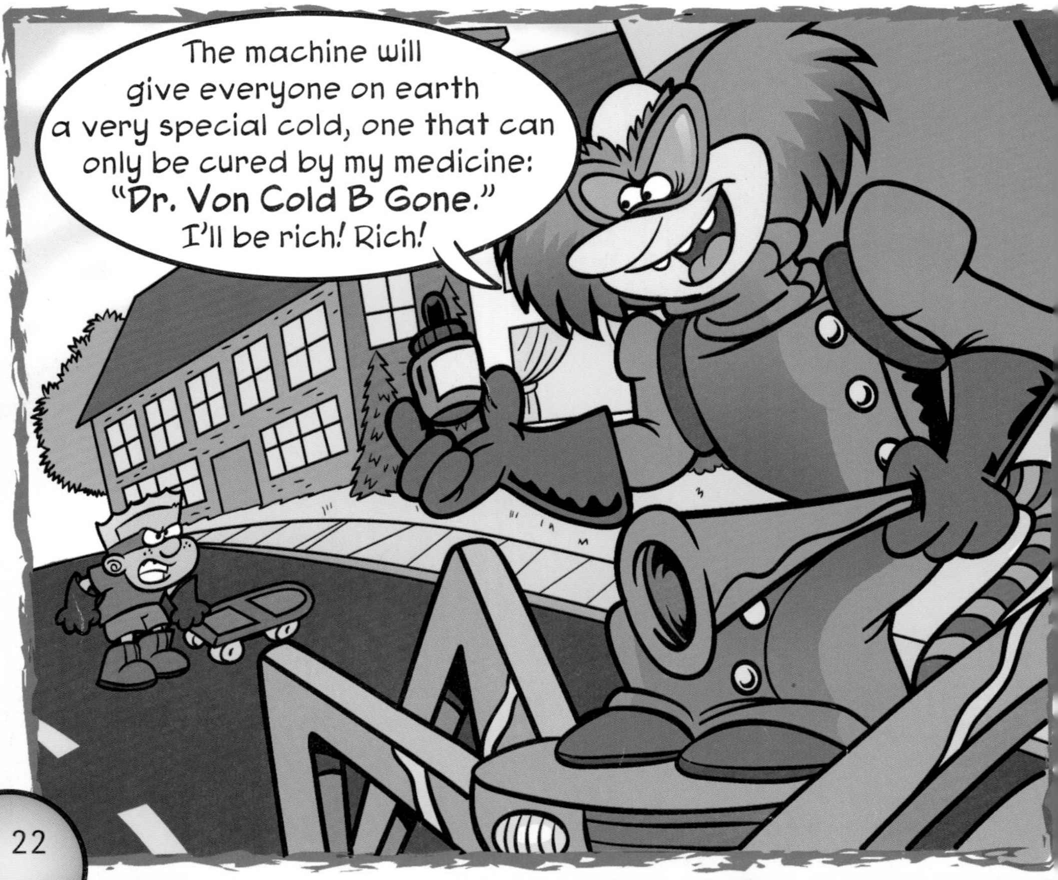
The machine will give everyone on earth a very special cold, one that can only be cured by my medicine: "**Dr. Von Cold B Gone.**" I'll be rich! Rich!

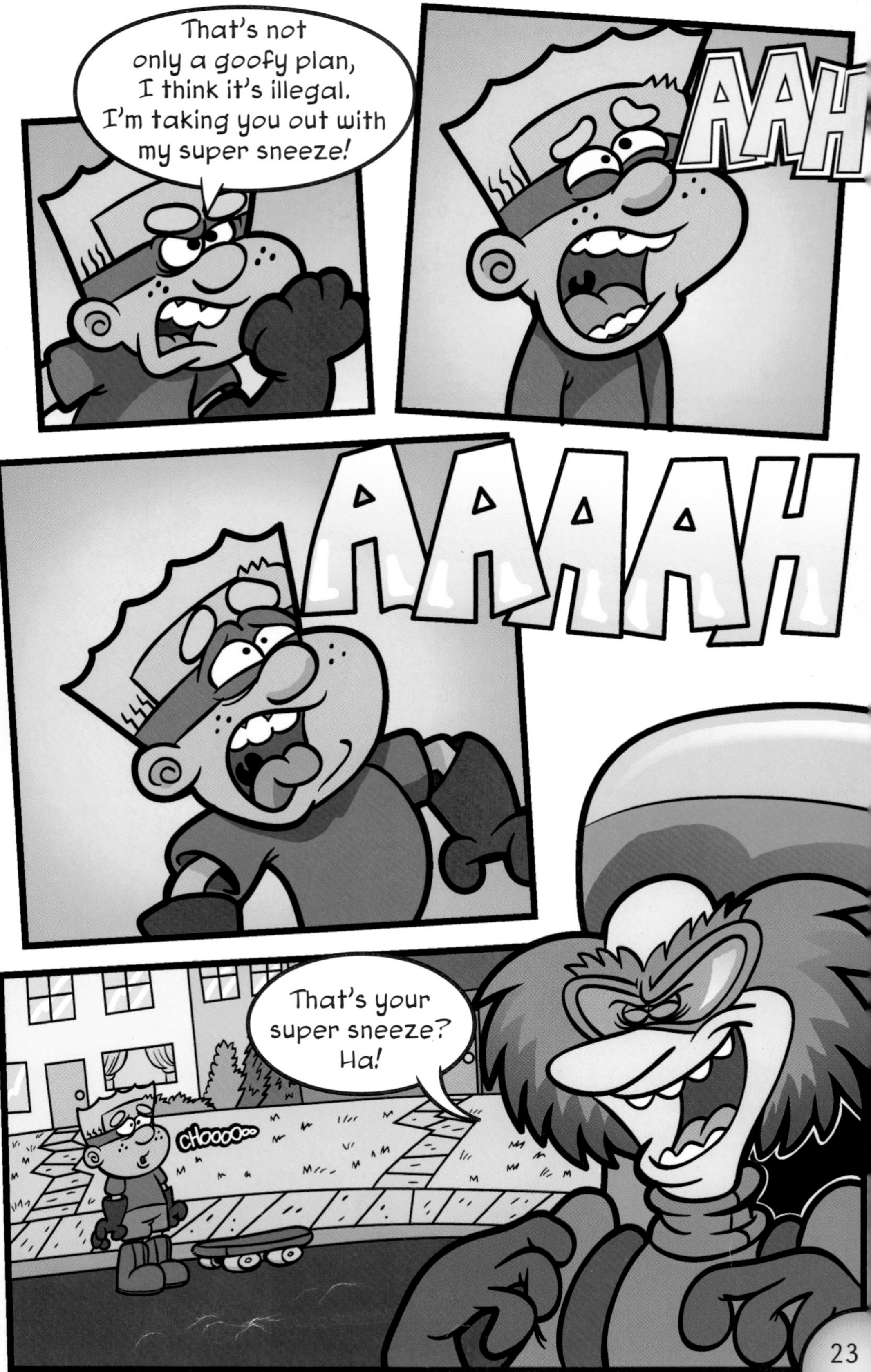
That's not only a goofy plan, I think it's illegal. I'm taking you out with my super sneeze!
AAH
AAAAH
CHOOOOoo
That's your super sneeze? Ha!

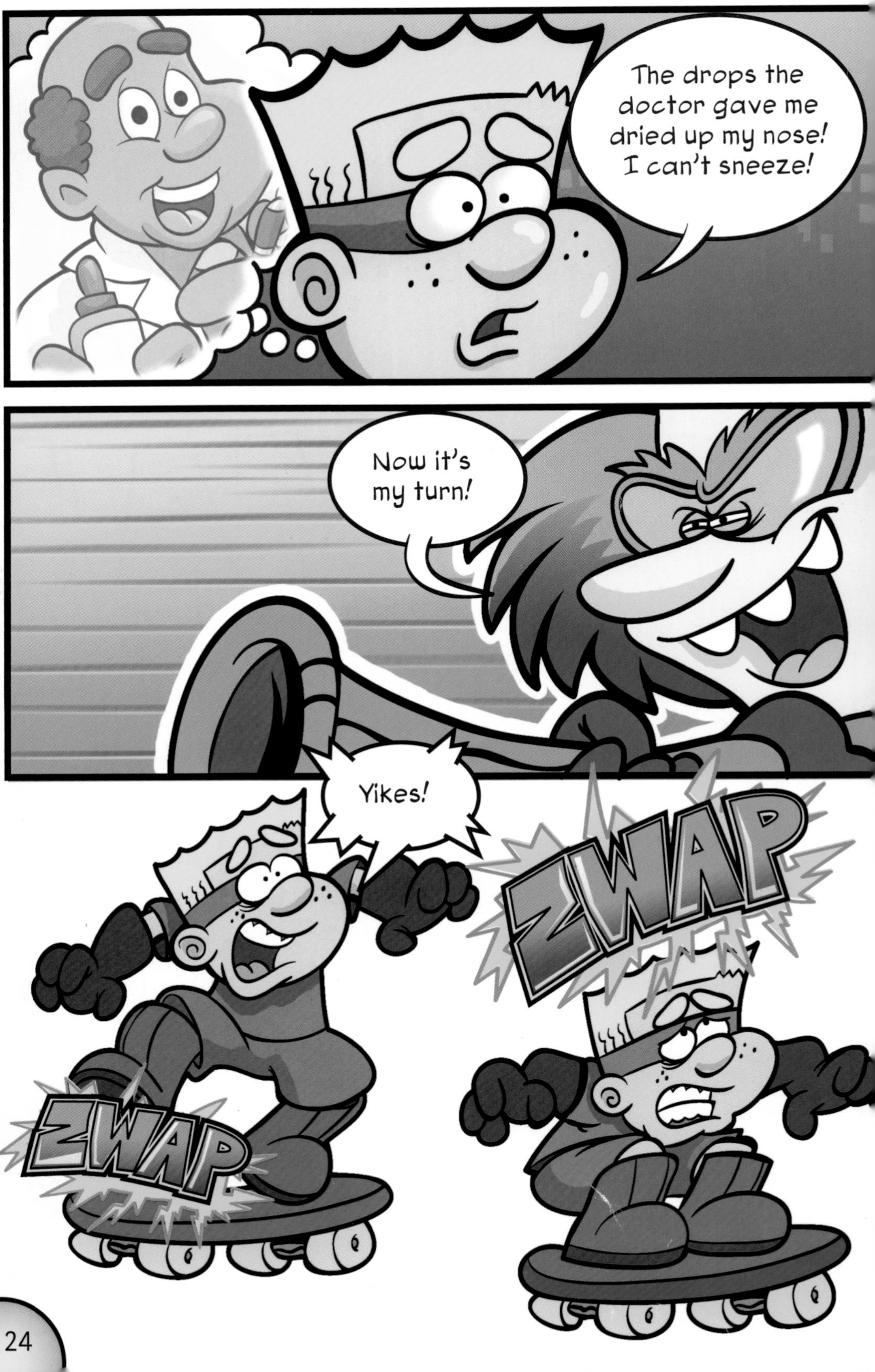
The drops the doctor gave me dried up my nose! I can't sneeze!
Now it's my turn!
Yikes!
ZWAP
ZWAP

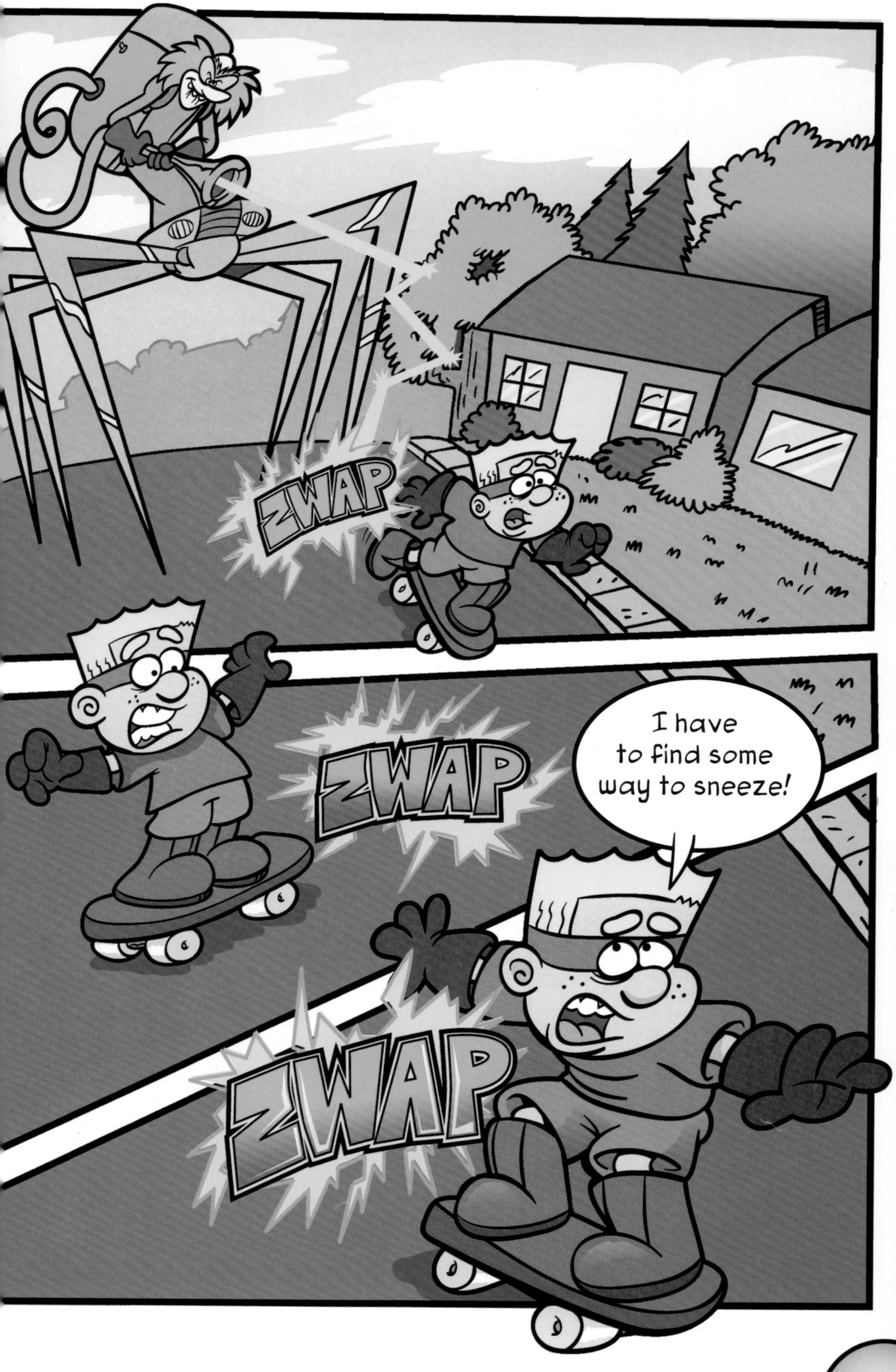
ZWAP
ZWAP
ZWAP
I have to find some way to sneeze!

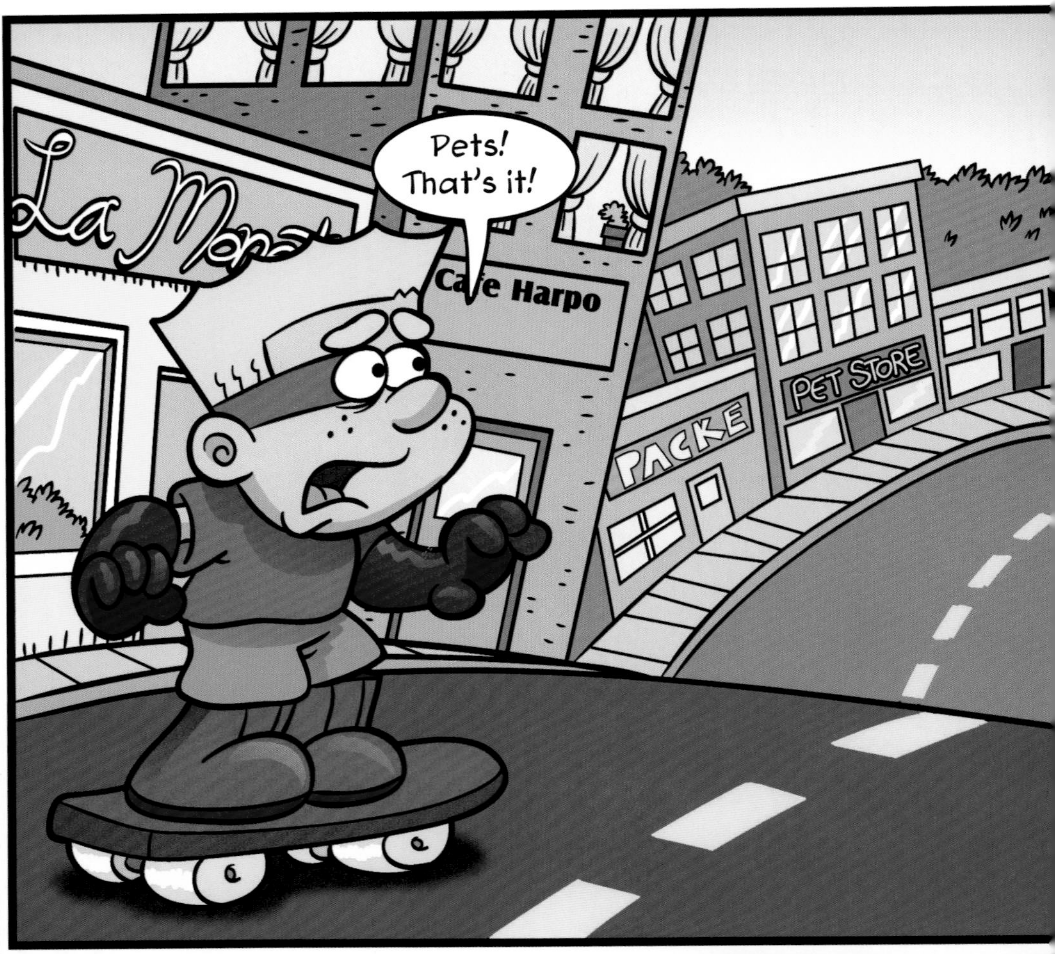
La Mona
Pets! That's it!
Cafe Harpo
PACKE
PET STORE

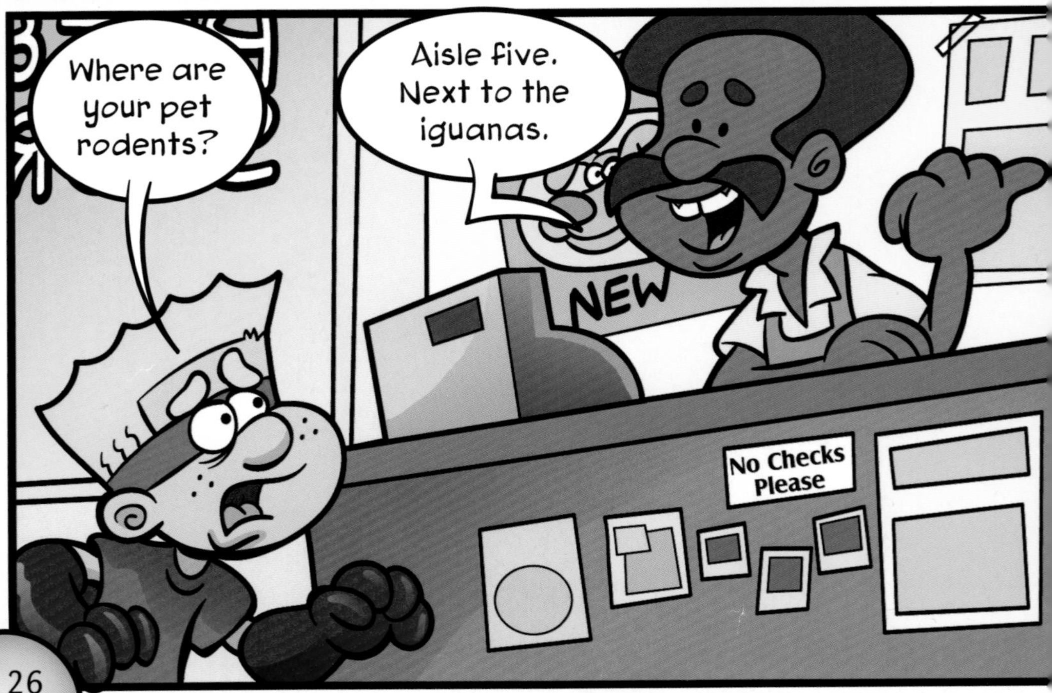
Where are your pet rodents?
Aisle five. Next to the iguanas.
NEW
No Checks Please

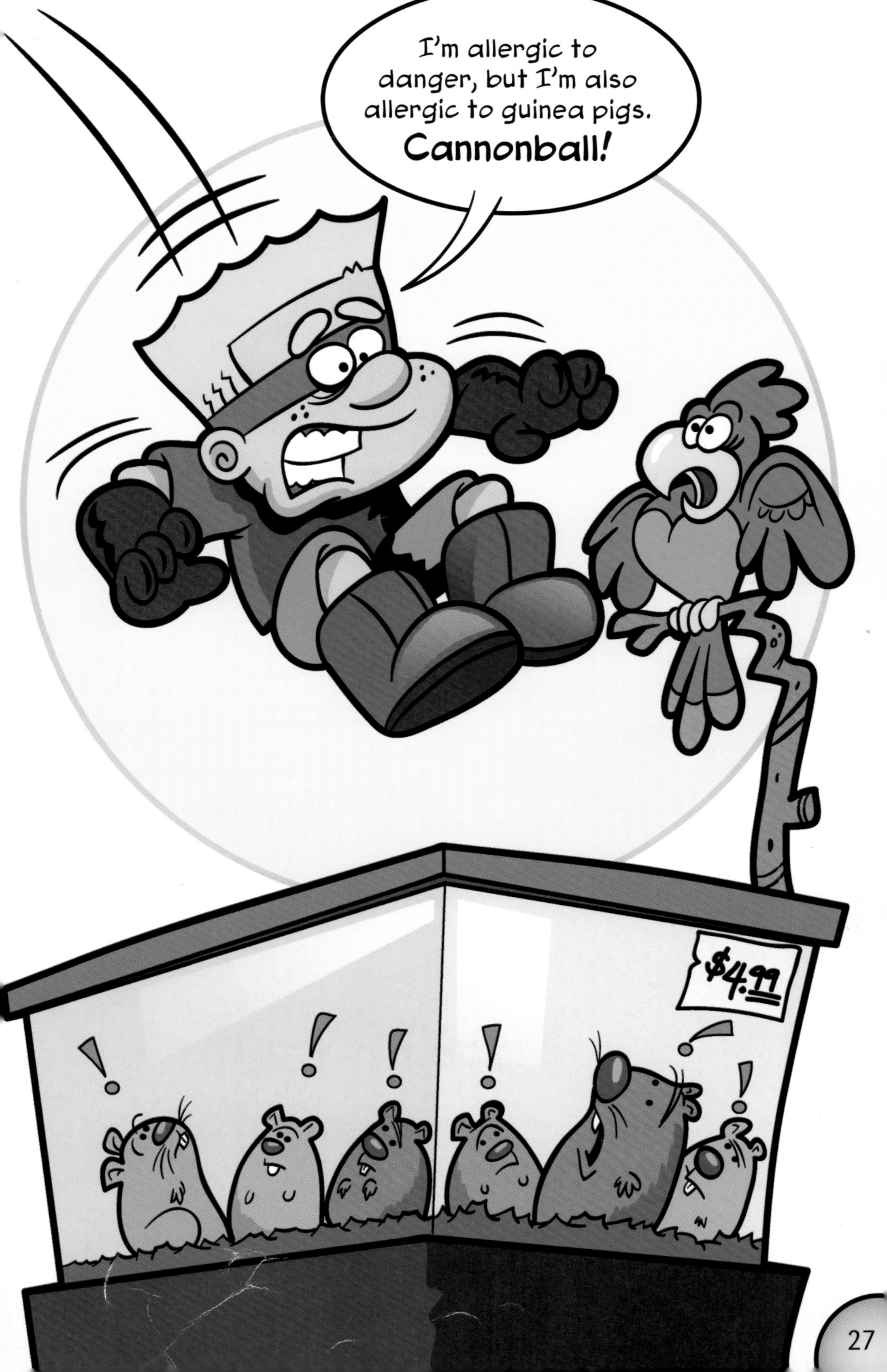
I'm allergic to danger, but I'm also allergic to guinea pigs.
Cannonball!
$4.99

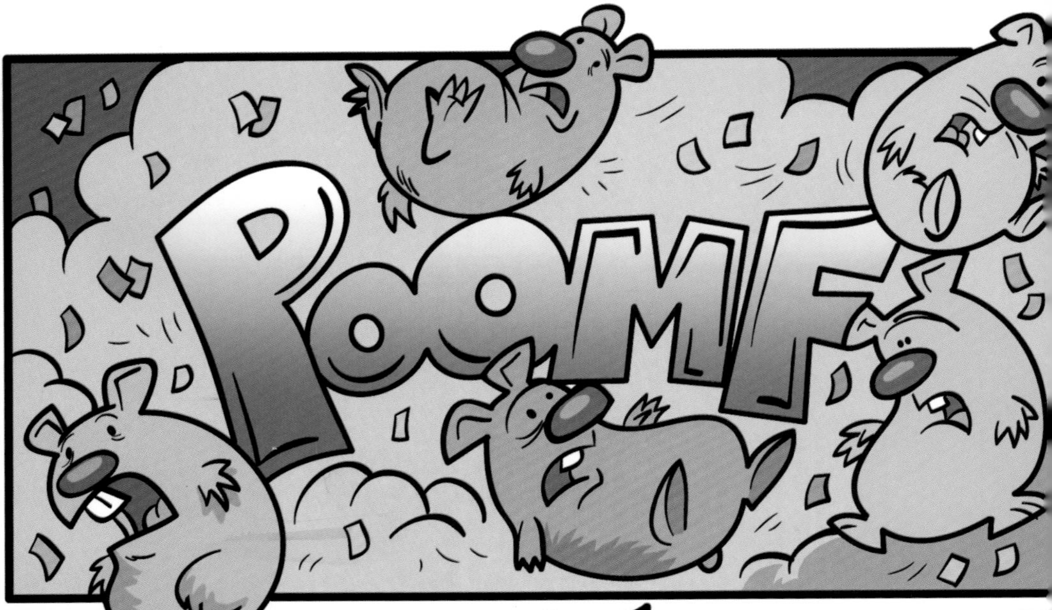
POOMF

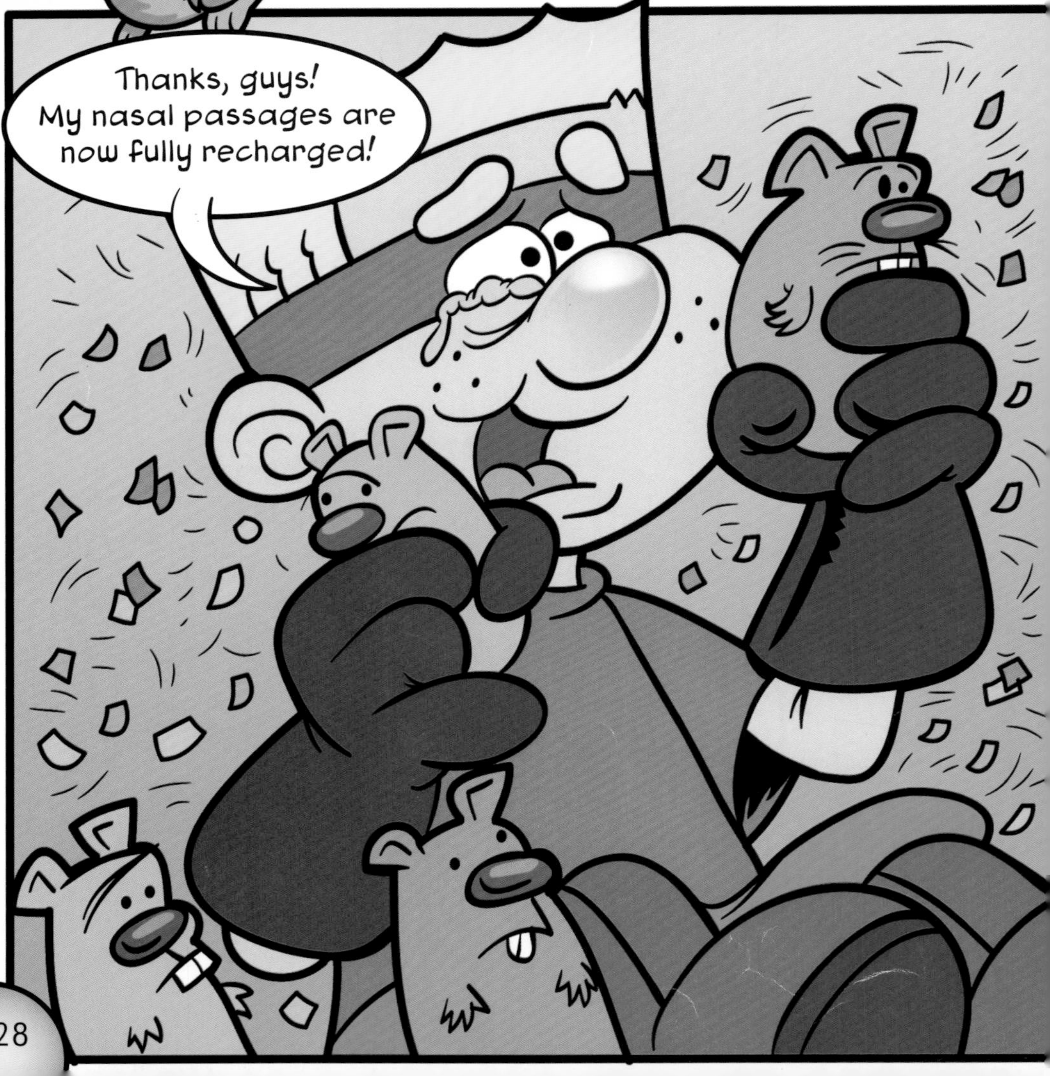
Thanks, guys!
My nasal passages are
now fully recharged!

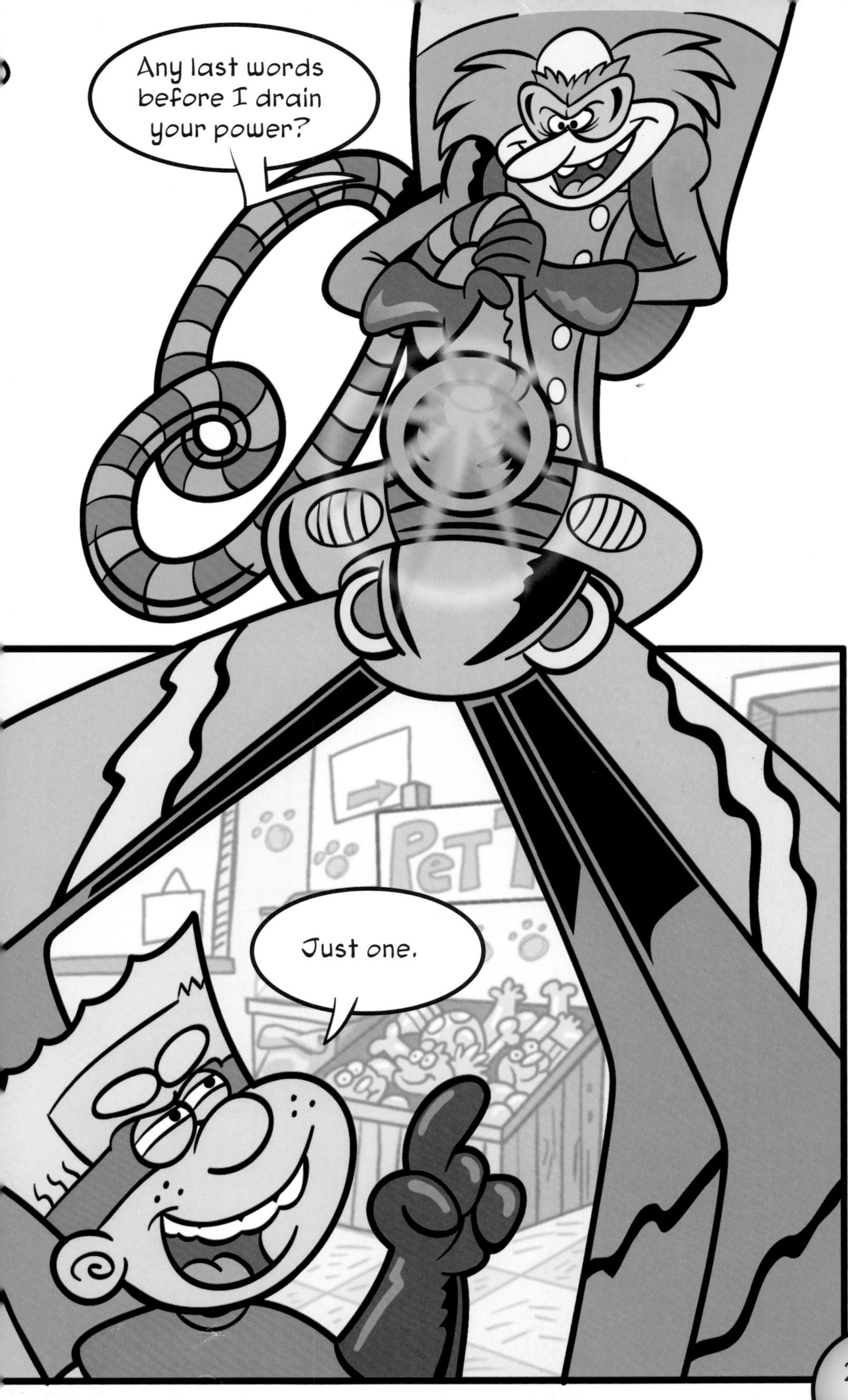
Any last words before I drain your power?
PeT
Just one.

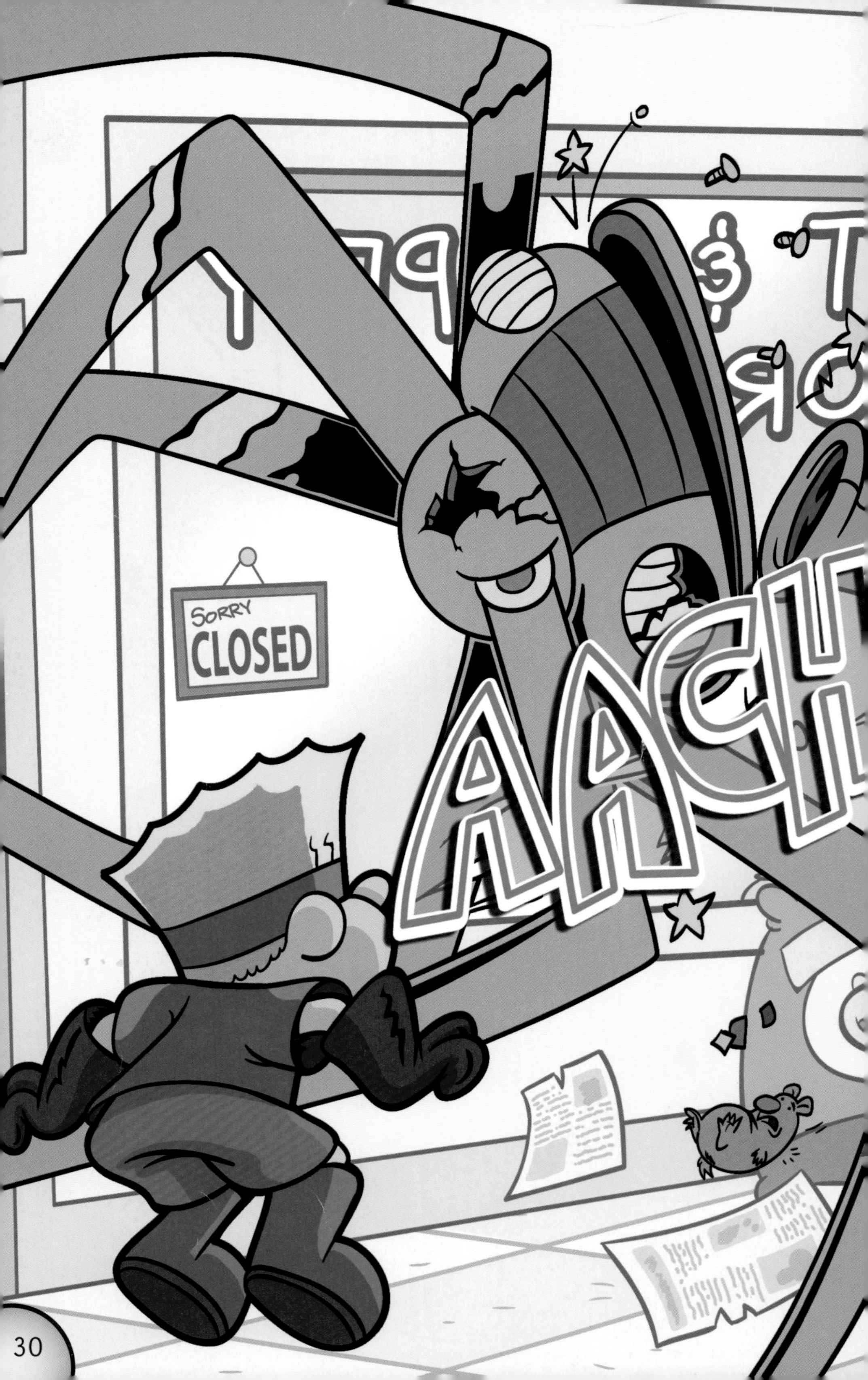
SORRY
CLOSED
AACH

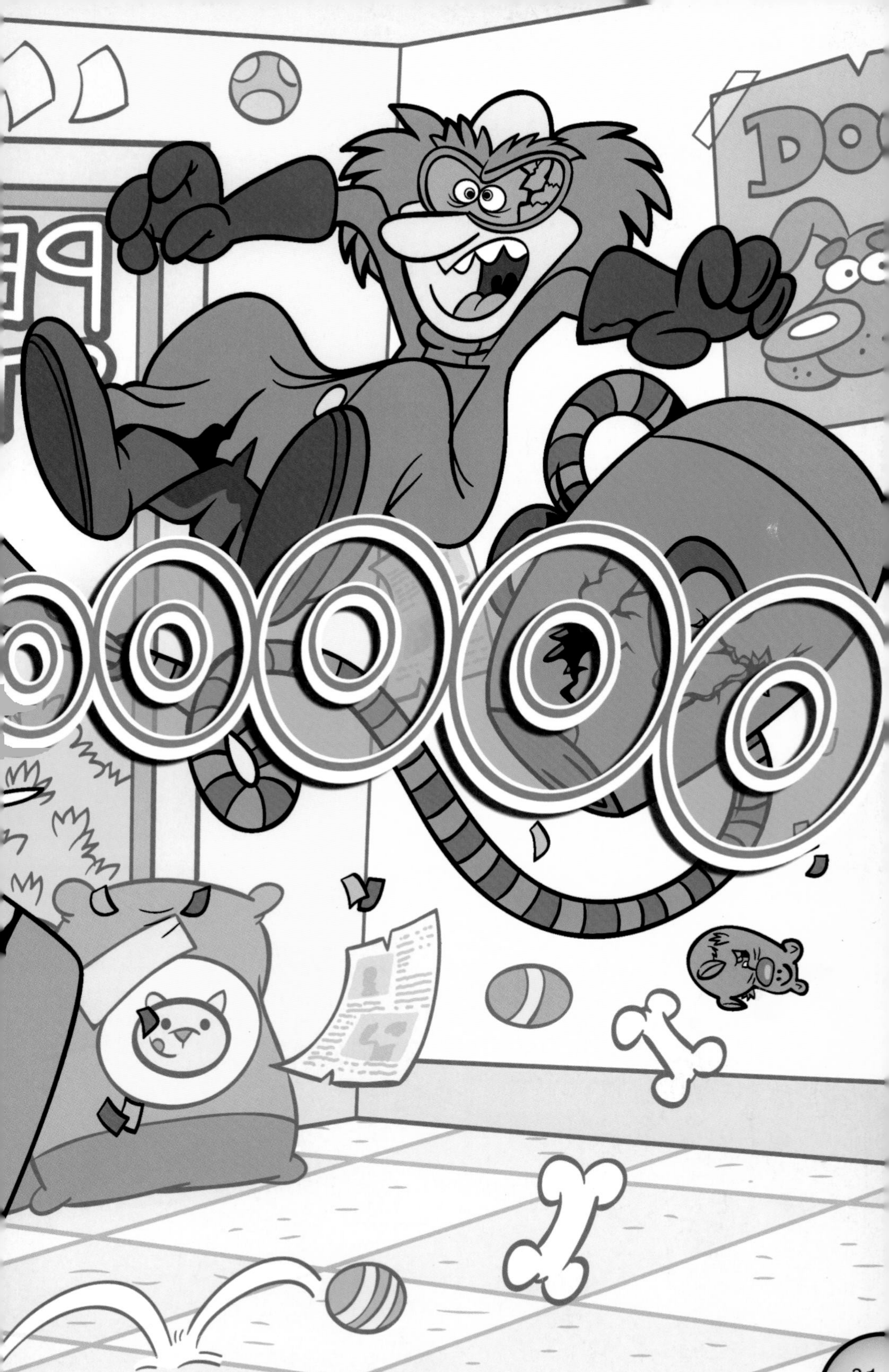
OOOOOO

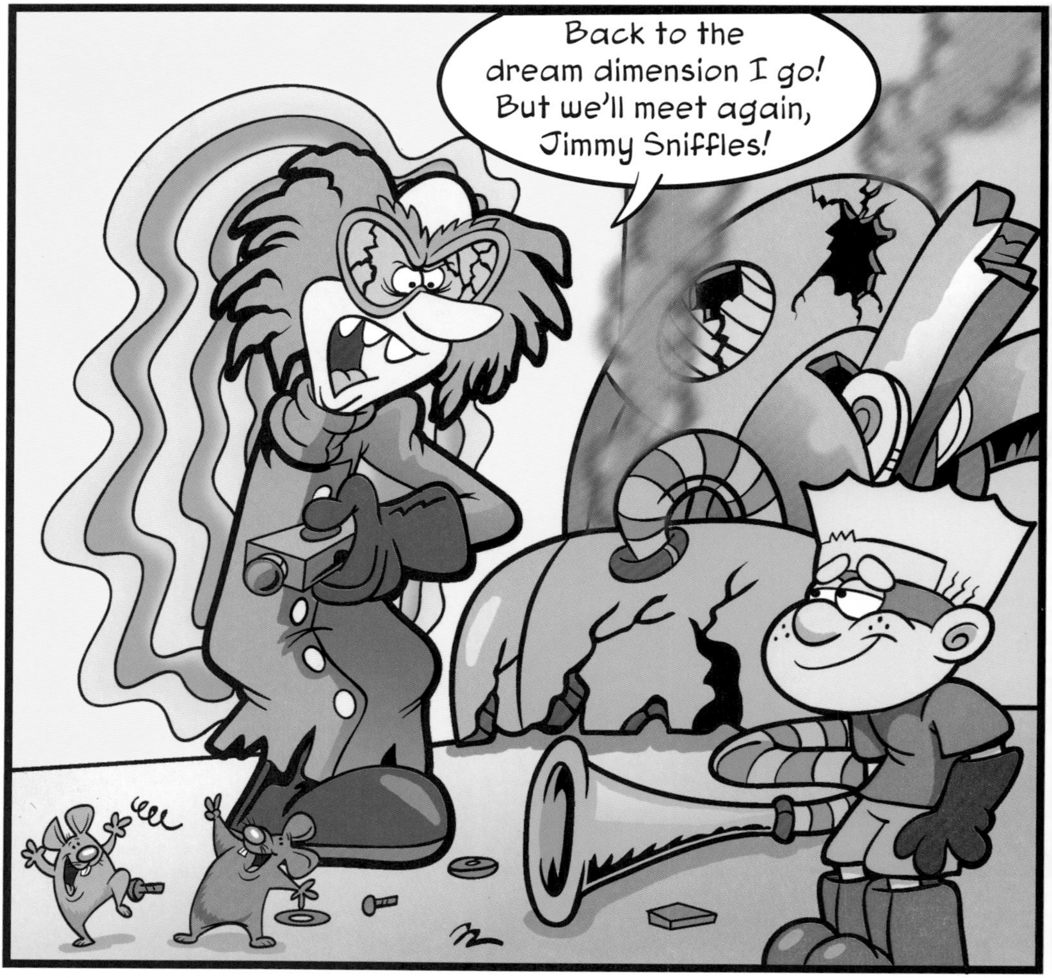
Back to the dream dimension I go! But we'll meet again, Jimmy Sniffles!

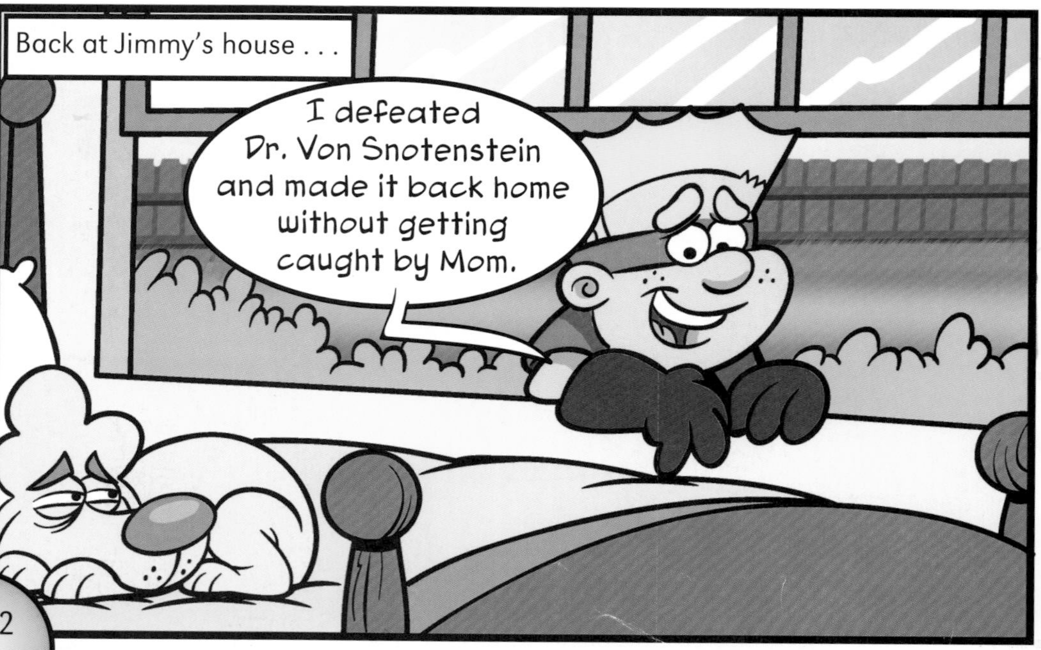
Back at Jimmy's house . . .
I defeated Dr. Von Snotenstein and made it back home without getting caught by Mom.

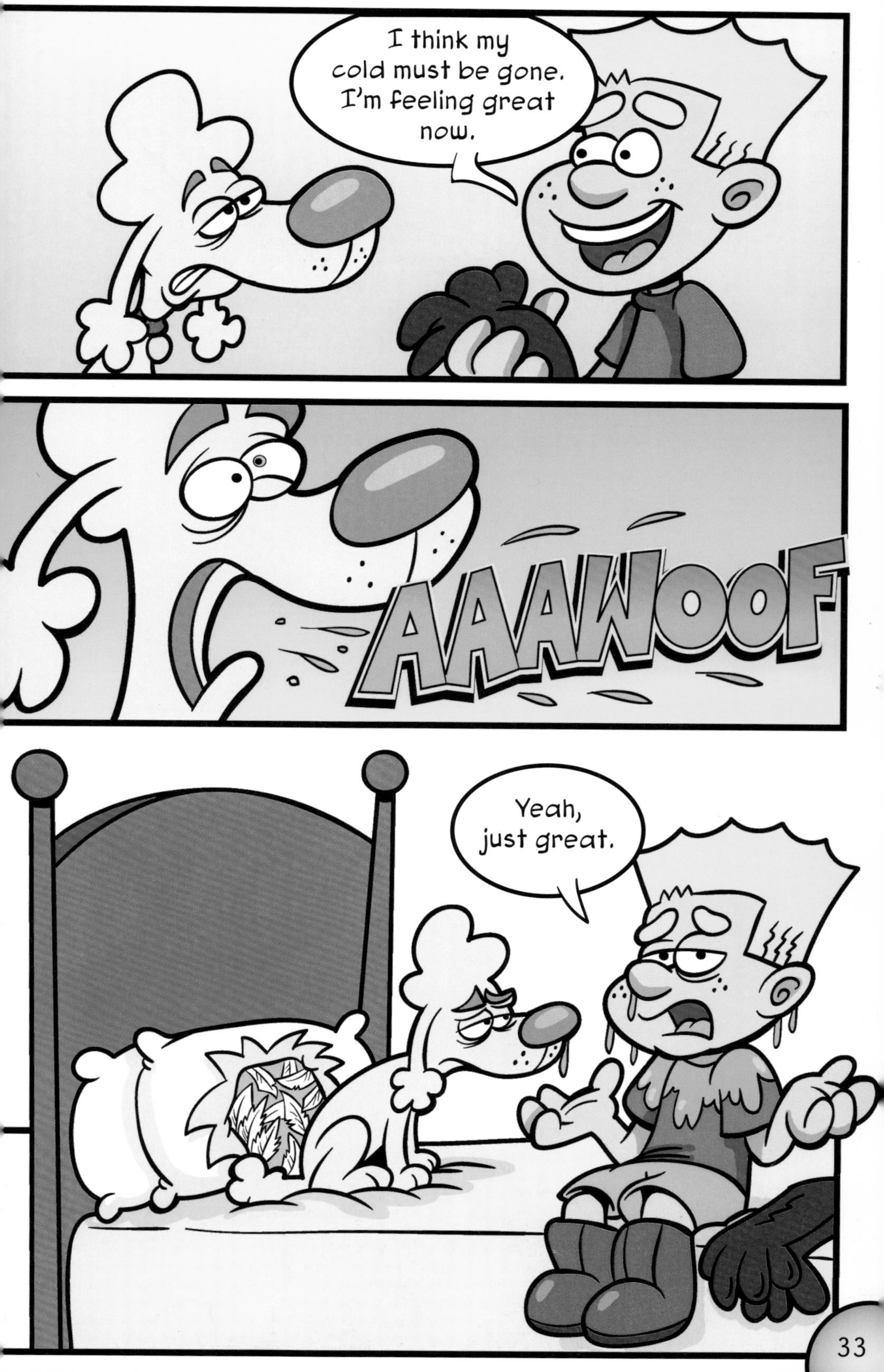
I think my cold must be gone. I'm feeling great now.
AAAWOOF
Yeah, just great.

ABOUT THE AUTHOR

Born in 1962 in Denver, Colorado, Scott Nickel
works by day at Paws, Inc., Jim Davis's famous
Garfield studio, and he freelances by night. Burning
the midnight oil, Scott has created hundreds of
humorous greeting cards and written several
children's books, short fiction for *Boys' Life*
magazine, comic strips, and lots of really funny
knock-knock jokes. He was raised in Southern
California, but in 1995 Scott moved to Indiana,
where he currently lives with his wife, two sons, six
cats, and several sea monkeys.

ABOUT THE ILLUSTRATOR

Steve Harpster has loved drawing funny cartoons,
mean monsters, and goofy gadgets since he was
able to pick up a pencil. In first grade, instead
of writing a report about a dog-sled story set in
Alaska, Steve made a comic book about it. He was
worried the teacher might not like it, but she hung
it up for all the kids in the class to see. "It taught
me to take a chance and try something different,"
says Steve. Steve landed a job drawing funny
pictures for books. He used to be an animator for
Disney. Now, Steve lives in Columbus, Ohio, with his
wonderful wife, Karen, and their sheepdog, Doodle.

GLOSSARY

allergic (ah-LUR-jik)—if you are allergic to things, you might sneeze, cough, or get a rash. People can be allergic to plants, dust, furry animals, or evil supervillains.

archenemy (arch-EN-uh-mee)—someone's very worst enemy

dimension (duh-MEN-shun)—an environment or surrounding where things live and move

radar (RAY-dar)—a cool, high-tech way to find objects by using invisible radio waves. Radar cannot be used, however, to find missing homework.

rodents (ROH-duntz)—small furry creatures with sharp front teeth for cutting and chewing. Rodents make good pets, unless you are a tree.

schnozz (shnahz)—a funny word for the nose. Other good words for nose are **beak**, **bazoo**, **honker**, **snoot**, and **whiffer**.

ultimate (UL-tuh-mit)—the most, or best, or biggest of something. An ultimate rodent would have a giant schnozz, and if it was allergic to humans, it would have a monster sneeze. ACHOO!

SNIFFLES ON SNEEZES

Teachers hate sneezes! Why? Because, according to some experts, students with colds and sniffles miss about 189 million school days each year!

The most famous sneeze on record took place on January 7, 1894. That's when inventor Thomas Edison made one of the world's first movies — about a man sneezing!

We humans sneeze to get rid of bad stuff in our bodies. The brain can sense a lump of mucus in our nose when we have a cold or an allergy. The body knows it shouldn't be there, so it tries to expel, or reject, the mucus with a powerful, eye-watering sneeze.

There is no cure for the common cold.

Gingerbread was an invention of the ancient Greeks. Long ago, the Chinese borrowed the recipe and used it as a medicine for colds. It didn't work, but it sure tasted good!

Be glad that you didn't have a cold in ancient Rome. The Romans use to treat their sneezes by soaking an onion in hot water and then drinking the mixture. Eeeew!

How fast is a sneeze? The average sneeze travels at about 100 miles per hour. According to some scientists, people sometimes blurt out a super-sneeze at 630 miles per hour. Yikes! Get out of the way!

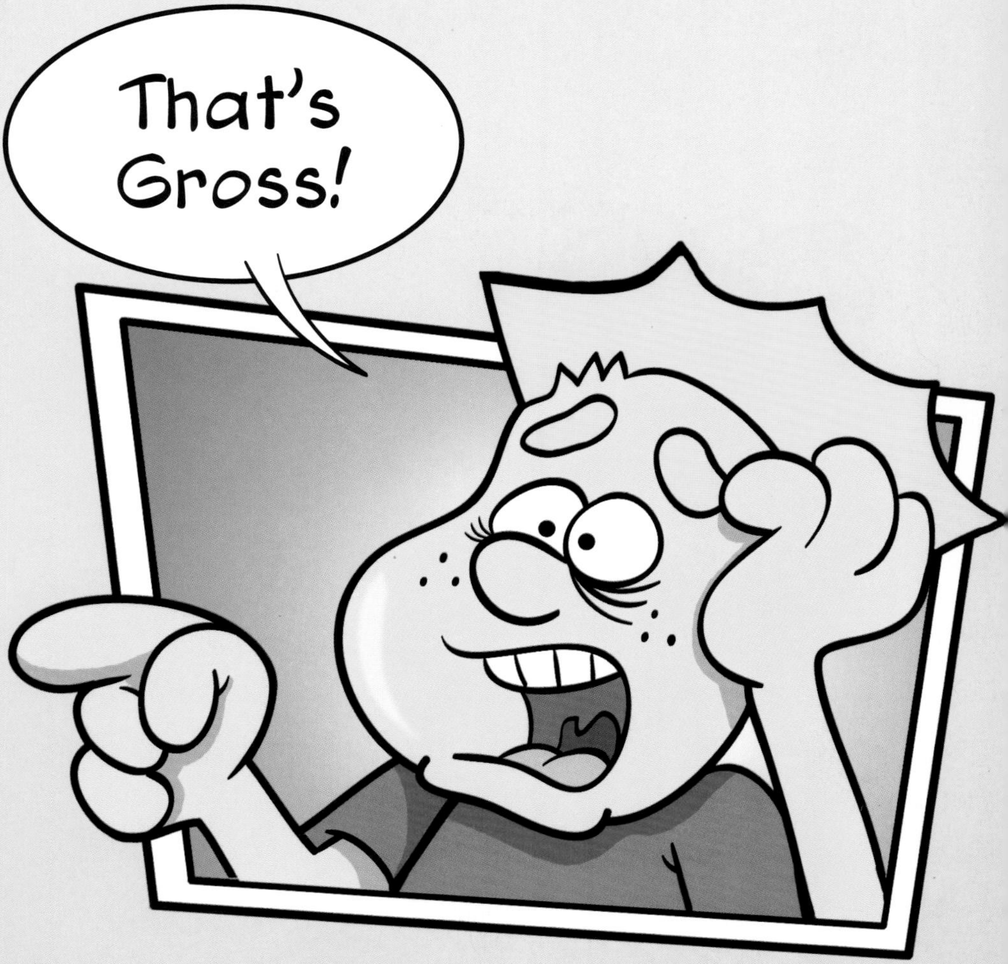
That's Gross!

DISCUSSION QUESTIONS

1. What is your favorite way to spend the day when you're home sick from school? Is there anything special that you do? Would you rather be home sick, or at school? Why?

2. Can you think of anything else Jimmy could have done to make himself sneeze?

3. Why does Dr. Von Snotenstein want to give everyone a cold that only his medicine can cure?

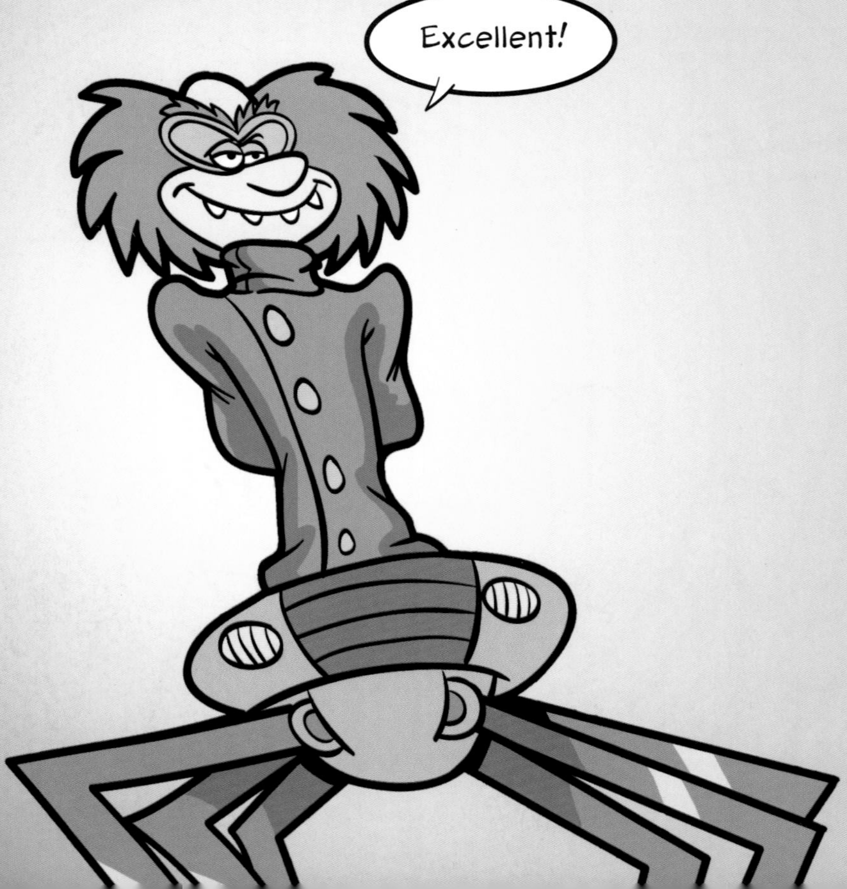
Excellent!

WRITING PROMPTS

1. Dr. Von Snotenstein is Jimmy's archenemy. Create your own evil character. What does he or she look like? What does he or she want to do? How would you defeat him or her?

2. Jimmy has a very interesting superpower, which is the ability to smell danger. If you could have any superpower, what would it be? What would you use it for?

3. Dr. Von Snotenstein creates some evil inventions. But not all inventions are used for evil. Create your own invention. Describe how it works, what it's made out of, and of course, what it is used for. And if you're feeling especially creative, draw a picture of it, too.

INTERNET SITES

Do you want to know more about subjects related to this book? Or are you interested in learning about other topics? Then check out FactHound, a fun, easy way to find Internet sites.

Our investigative staff has already sniffed out great sites for you!

Here's how to use FactHound:

1. Visit *www.facthound.com*

2. Select your grade level.

3. To learn more about subjects related to this book, type in the book's ISBN number: 1598894110.

4. Click the **Fetch It** button.

FactHound will fetch the best Internet sites for you!